Summer People

Summer People

Janice Elliott

HODDER AND STOUGHTON
LONDON SYDNEY AUCKLAND TORONTO

PR
6055
L48
S9

British Library Cataloguing in Publication Data
Elliott, Janice
  Summer People
  I. Title
  823'.9'1F   PR6055.L48s/

  ISBN 0 340 25172 7

For Caroline

1

So THE SEASON opens and the usual crowd fling into their estate wagons bags and dogs and cats and children and potties and swimsuits and tennis rackets and sleeping bags and hamsters. And take off as they always do at this time of year for the coast. Holidays are long now – so much has changed in the few short years since 1984 came and went without cosmic disaster – and some of the men can get the whole summer. They are lucky to have their houses by the sea on this Atlantic, western shore, where summers nowadays are hotter, though winters more bitter.

Just as the van is packed and Bea and Herman Tyler are ready to go – Toby starting the journey on the front bench seat between his parents, though later he will seek a nest in the back for his long legs – the telephone rings in the house.

Herman groans.

'Can't we leave it?' says Bea.

As each parent speaks Toby swivels his head like a tennis umpire.

Herman: 'Perhaps it's for the Catarullas' – the American academic couple, unseen but recommended, who have rented the house for the summer.

Bea: 'We're all locked up.'

An old dog with stiff joints raises a quivering leg against the red antique post-box at the corner under the bursting, dusty lime: he looks embarrassed, like an incontinent geriatric of sound mind but treacherous bladder. The Tylers think how glad they will be to get out of town: suddenly it seems a dreadful place, especially to Bea who loves the sea – their stretch of coast at least – even more than does Herman.

7

Though she appreciates the fact that it is possible to walk about at night in the capital, still, without being mugged. As a rule. So far.

Herman: 'Maybe we'd better answer it.'

'You want to answer it?'

'I never said I wanted to answer it.'

'I could answer it,' says Toby, and Bea and Herman look startled, as though they had suddenly been confronted by this seventeen-year-old gangly boy, their son, delivered complete and sharp at the elbows.

'No,' says Herman, with bravado. 'Let it ring.'

The telephone goes on ringing in the empty house and then stops, like a crying child that has suddenly been silenced.

Perhaps Herman is worried about the unanswered telephone, because when they are held up at lights or a level crossing or in a traffic jam, he drums his finger tips on the wheel. Bea nudges Toby and dips her head in Herman's direction meaning: your father's fidgety since he stopped smoking. (This is an old game Bea and her son have played for years, a family ritual, but lately Toby has not enjoyed it so much. He is not sure if he feels embarrassed for his father or less happy than he used to be in the role of conspirator, however benevolent. As an only child, he has always taken it for granted that he is closer to his parents than most children. They have in a sense been his siblings, he is beginning to realise that, and wonders – without quite formulating the idea – what the form is when you cast off your father and mother if they happen also to be your brother and sister? He isn't fretting yet. He assumes things will work themselves out.)

There is Bea in jeans and shirt, a small, neat woman with pretty hair, looking more like a girl than her forty-five years. Not that she has ever strained after youthfulness, she simply has a useful metabolism.

There are burners and storers, apparently, and Bea happens to be a burner.

Perhaps that had something to do with the miscarriages. Though probably not. Anyway Bea has never worried about Timbo (Toby) being the only one, and she never had imperial maternal ambitions. Everyone says how nice he has turned out and all the problems she expected have never cropped up.

Bea has other worries. A slight frown that may age her. Nothing to do with Toby.

No potties for the Tylers to unpack. Not for years now – yet here, by the sea, that time doesn't seem so far away: there are shards of Timbo's childhood that have not been thrown out, a one-armed Action Man half-buried in the dune beyond the garden, a broken go-cart he might mend some day for one of the summer children, a model yacht Herman gave him when he was too young, and by the time he was old enough, Timbo was sailing a real boat; all these, thinks Bea, who has dabbled in archaeology (though palaeontology is her passion), are *objets trouvés* and as such have magic and therefore cannot be thrown out. Magic for Timbo, she means, though she would miss them too. Toby is not so sure. This year, in particular, he is by no means certain that he appreciates the preservation of relics but for Bea's sake he can't bring himself to dispose of them. This year there is a kind of watching politeness between Toby and his parents.

This is different from every other year. Toby is old enough now to go off with his own friends, in fact there was some talk about the Club Méditerranée or hitching to Spain (though hitching in Europe is not so easy these days on account of the violence). Then they might all have gone abroad together but Herman wasn't keen, he travels so much. Then there would be the usual crowd at the sea, their friends, and the beach-house: a shame not to use it. They catch their first sniff of the sea. They are determined to enjoy themselves. There are dreadful things going on in the world, whole continents coming up to the boil, the polar cap melting, the economy of the west collapsing, civil war in Ireland, the American president assassinated (again), civil war in Africa, genocide here, genocide there, crazy prices, fall-out in milk, radioactive leaks, terrorists absolutely everywhere and it's not much better out in space, either, with laser beams and spy satellites. But not one of the Tylers is going to say: this may be the last summer.

The house is white clapboard, facing a sea that can be violent, so in the autumn they put up storm shutters; shingle is tossed into the garden and the salt finds its way even behind the storm shutters – until they are cleaned the windows will be blind. There is rime everywhere the salt wind can reach, like the crust that gathers around the eyes in sleep. Even upon the Willings's house and they are winter people, they stay here all the year round.

They go through the house opening it up. Herman and Toby have struggled with the storm shutters and humped most of the luggage indoors.

Bea stands hugging a blanket at the window of Toby's room, which has two bunk beds and is designed rather like the cabin of a boat.

'Look,' she says, 'you can see the lighthouse.' In the sea-light her face looks tired, but, of course, it's been a long journey. She sighs and drops the blanket on the bed. 'Did you know? It's not manned any more.'

Bea goes round the house, touching her things, bringing them to life. They have peanut-butter sandwiches and beer at the kitchen table.

Bea moves things around on the table. She mentions the lighthouse.

Herman looks up from his book, at last. He seems distracted, a dog looking for its basket, he's been edgy all day.

'Lighthouses are going automatic,' he says. 'There's something wrong with the waste-disposal. You'd better get Cudlipp in.'

'If he's still alive.'

'Why shouldn't he be alive?'

'Cudlipp was old,' says Bea. 'People die.'

Toby looks at his mother and his father.

He notices (though this has gone on for years) that it is always Bea who has to get people in, like plumbers and builders and glaziers and doctors and vets and policemen both times they were burgled. His father has always kept himself above such things. Toby wonders if his mother minds. You can't tell. She has always been good with people; workmen, strangers on trains and planes, hard cases. Bea is a collector of lame dogs, though this may be involuntary. Sometimes she seems to help them, just as she puts together broken sea-birds (my mother mends sea-gulls, Toby had once written in a school essay when he was seven or eight or nine); in summer there is always a tern or a gull or a cormorant moping in the cage on the lawn. When he was small, trying to imitate her secretly, Toby was responsible for a few deaths.

Bea lights a cigarette. She has never even tried to give up, though she's down to low tar king-size filter-tip.

'Even the off-shore ones?' She's still on lighthouses.

Toby drops his beer can in the pedal bin. While he's at the sink in this modern fully automatic kitchen (not inhuman: there's a stripped pine dresser, a row of oilskins on hooks and some pretty crockery), he tries the waste-disposal switch. Then the fan.

'The waste-disposal's not working because the electricity's turned off,' he says.

His mother and father seem amazed.

There was a time when Toby used to be afraid his parents might die. His father fall out of an aeroplane. His mother get cancer. This was a real, urgent fear. Violent images possessed him. Whenever they left the house he felt they might never return, they were going into danger.

Another time he wished his father dead and sweated like a murderer till Herman came home looking much the same as usual.

People die.

Bea stays on in the kitchen, thinking she might make cottage cheese this year. Although the journey is over she has not yet truly arrived: some small ritual, she knows, will correct this condition and then she may reclaim her house. Meanwhile it is not unpleasant to drift. Through the kitchen window she can see her son on the beach: long-legged, kicking around in the shingle with his hands in his pockets, a little round-shouldered, as if his height and his thinness made him stoop, the same hair as hers: crinkly, an indeterminate fairish colour that darkens in winter and in summer looks streaky. In the unsummerly wind (though the sun, in an edgy way, is brilliant) Toby wears jeans, of course, and a thin denim shirt, faded and patched. Well, he wears jeans all year, winter too, and claims not to be cold, even when his hands feel icy. Once Timbo was so sweet and warm, somewhere between five and ten. That was gone so fast and yet it lasted for a long time. Then there was a strange jerk and time seemed to race.

The cat is cross, stalks high-legged round the kitchen, affronted by this trauma of journey and house-changing, will not be consoled. It does not like sea-smells, though sometimes it slopes off to the estuary where they bring in the mackerel, on cat business. Since it is neutered, it was probably a fish-fight with some rough sea-Tom that sent it home with a piece of ear chewed off. The cat's fishy business can be revolting: like the time it strolled into one of the Tylers' rare semi-posh parties and dumped the remains of something unspeakable – tail, spine and head with bulging eyes – on the only good rug.

The end of its tail quivers with rage. The cat won't touch milk. Bea tips the last of her beer into a saucer and puts it on the floor.

'Oh, cat, you are appalling.'

They never bought it or even chose it. It simply walked into the house on a rainy night, soaked, starveling and furious, its ribs like those of a ship whose hull has been eaten by termites. They never named it.

'One of your lame cats?' said Herman.

Oh, all these violent, doomed and dangerous creatures, thinks Bea – why do they always turn up at my door? But then, she supposes, she would not be without them. Known for her kindness: what an epitaph. Timbo must be somewhere still inside that razor-boned person skimming stones out there, that stranger on the beach; she doesn't fret about it but thinks of Toby, of course, and in her mind's eye nowadays her son's face is always just averted. Only in dreams is he quite unguarded, as he had truly been for a while. Well, at least he's not a monster. She must be lucky. She supposes.

Bea thinks she will put off unpacking. She has remembered the ritual that will help, and is smiling already as she finds the key under the tea-cosy and opens the magical drawer, and there they all are, her amateurish uninformed collection. Palaeontology, she thinks, lovely word. Ammonites, Gastropoda, Cephalopoda, Strophomenids. Why not delight in them? She never had daughters.

'Coo-ee?'

Lord, she might have known: the Be Happy note stuck with sellotape on the parcel box. Foxgloves in a bucket on the porch.

Erin Willings bearing a chicken casserole with too much garlic for Herman flops down in the basket chair. Erin is probably Bea's best friend, or at least they have known one another a long time, ever since the usual crowd started coming here in summer.

Erin looks like a Henry Moore that has taken life, stomped out of the exhibition and stuffed herself on pasta, between giving birth to a legion. If she could relax in her amplitude she really would be a Moore woman, beautiful and full, an ovoid materfamilias. But Erin is what they call nowadays at dinner parties in the city and in the psychology department of Western University where she works, a smiling depressive. That is, while your common or garden depressive is recognisably glum, inturned, cheerful as Eeyore's birthday party, Erin offers the world a Charley Brown smile: if you stick to her mouth you can quite forget that she is perfectly capable of killing herself.

'I can't tell you,' she says to Bea, 'thank God you're here. It's so lovely to see you. Oh, my God, it's so lovely.'

The trouble with Erin, Herman remarked in one of his rare abrasive moods, is that she's a Henry Moore married to a Frink. There is some truth in this, as there is in many shallow remarks. Merlyn Willings, in a mid-Atlantic Celtic way, is a warrior, a horseman stern and distant. Bea wonders what attracted Erin to him in the first place and decides it must have been that she hoped to be stormed, to be swept up and borne away. Only to discover that the man in the iron mask had but a single interest: American fiction in the latter half of the twentieth century – upon which he instructs his students with a passion the nubile females find disturbing.

Bea thinks Erin thinks Merlyn believes her, Erin, to be an idiot. Erin is probably right. Merlyn, too, might be right, but Bea prefers not to think about this, because Erin is her friend.

'It's lovely to be here.' Bea offers Erin a beer. 'Sorry, no coffee. The electricity's off. I tried the switch in the cupboard there, but nothing happened. There must be some muddle. Last year we got your bill, remember?'

'Oh Lord, yes,' Erin groans, 'we *eat* electricity.'

There is a pause. The two women drink and smoke. Soon Bea will ring SeaLec and sort out the muddle, then the electricity will be returned to them, they can boil the kettle, re-stock the deep freeze, turn on the lights and the television and the mixer and the waste-disposal, bring the house to life.

'How was the winter? How's Merlyn?'

'Malamud!' says Erin and bursts into tears.

Bea sits it out, which is the best way with Erin. While Erin gasps and chokes into Kleenex, Bea composes shopping lists in her head and remembers how lovely her friend was the first summer: encountered on the beach, stepping from the sea with her children, a big, beautiful furry girl with good white teeth. It was the children, of course, who brought them together, also, a little later, the need, just for a while, to be rid of the children. So, very daring, they left the Willings's au pair in charge and dashed off to the town where they drank in the best hotel and, in the town's first boutique, tried on, rather tipsily, some wild clothes. Until Erin giggled and gasped: for heaven's sake, d'you realise what we're doing? What we always do! *Shopping!* They bought some clothes but never wore them, and exchanged too many confidences. When they got back Erin's youngest had cut its knee and the au pair was in Belgian sulks. That was the first time Bea saw Erin cry.

'Updike wasn't so bad,' says Erin, drying out, 'but I can't cope with Malamud.'

'Who's Malamud?'

'An American novelist. A bit old fashioned. Everyone used to pretend they'd read him.'

Bea goes to the dresser and finds the bottle of brandy from last season, a little dusty (how can dust penetrate a sealed house? The same way the salt does, she supposes). She wipes a glass and pours a good slug for Erin, a small one for herself.

'Drink,' she says. Probably she shouldn't if Erin's on tranquillisers or anti-depressants. Oh well.

Erin manages a smile. 'Two ladies of a certain age getting plastered in the afternoon.'

Bea suddenly feels tired, from the journey, the unpacking, the day, Erin. 'I shouldn't think so. And we're not that old.'

'Actually,' Erin confides, 'now he's done with boring Bernard I think it might be John Hawkes next or Roth. I found them on his desk with next term's notes and peeked. I liked the Roth best, but they're both quite sexy.' The brandy's working. Erin is much better. 'You know what I once did, but don't tell Merlyn or he'll kill me.'

Bea looks politely interested. In a way she is interested but she would like to join Timbo on the beach and scavenge for pebbles or shells or flotsam as they used to do; sometimes they found the limbs of trees, wonderfully bleached and smoothed.

Erin is going to tell her anyway. 'Years ago I wrote to one of those blasted Americans – Bellow or Mailer or Heller or someone – and said: why don't you pull yourself together and go to pieces like a man. Thurber said that. I never got a reply because it was anonymous.'

'That's funny. That's very good.'

Erin's eyes are dangerously damp again. 'You know he went blind?'

'Bellow?'

'Thurber. Before he died, of course. How's darling Herman?'

'Herman's fine.'

'Timbo's so tall now! I saw him on the beach. He's a sweet boy. You're lucky, Bea.'

'Yes, I'm lucky.'

Suddenly, in that odd, exclusive female accord (though close married couples have it too), the two women are saying d'you remember? Do you remember when Timbo was three, four, five, when they'd leave the men to sail or work and spend the day with the children at fossil beach. The past is safe ground and rich. It may be the brandy, but quite soon they're laughing, and that is how Toby finds them. He stands there gangling in the doorway; every lintel nowadays seems too low for him. Bea's tall son. He is old enough to under-stand that the women, his mother and her friend, are not laughing at him. (For years now Bea's female friends have been confiding in Toby, even asking his advice. He never seemed to mind.)

'Hello, Erin.'

Toby has always got on well with Erin. He has brought in a Coke from the car and sits now, as he has often done before, with the two women in the kitchen. There might be a difference though, this summer. Toby smells of salt, there is rime already in his hair and later, if he swims, the sea and sun will stripe his pale hair green.

When he's finished the Coke he doesn't know what to do with his hands.

He hadn't meant to interrupt but Erin says: 'Well, I must be off. I suppose.' And when no one stops her: 'It's terrible what they're doing.'

Bea is puzzled, wondering where Herman is, tired. 'Doing?'

'Well the new houses were bad enough. But there's been some trouble lately. You know, those kids sleeping on the beach. They come and go.' Like Red Riding Hood about to enter the forest, she stands at the door with her basket. 'I should lock up anyway.'

'Thanks for the chicken.'

'Open house tonight, if you're not too tired? We ought to christen the season.'

'I'll have to ask Herman.'

Erin nods, leaves with a smile. 'Don't grow any more, Timbo boy. Bless you, Bea.'

For what, thinks Bea? Whatever have I ever done? She walks by the sea with Timbo for a while, just as she had imagined this holiday, and in a rock-pool they find a bird washed up.

'A gull?'

'No, a sea-swallow.' There is nothing even Bea can do. There are some birds that cannot be caged or cured. She touches its warm throat and detects a faltering pulse. There is no mark. The bright eyes close, the lids folding upwards. Though there is nothing they can do they stay with it until it dies, then they walk home along the beach.

Herman Tyler, meanwhile, having sat in his study but still found himself unable to shake off his keyed-up mood, has marched up to the head above fossil beach. He strides out, a large, good-looking, slightly clumsy man, with sandy hair and a tentative smile. He might be a farmer or a sailor but works, in fact, for a multinational corporation on whose behalf he is almost constantly airborne. In spite of his self-deprecating air, Herman is no fool; rather than a farmer or a sailor, he might, perhaps, in another world, have made one of the gentler colonial administrators – with sunburned knees dispensing justice from a canvas stool set before a table in a jungle clearing. As it is, he's in a hustling business and fears flying.

Before turning back Herman stands on the headland to catch his breath and watches the gale approach from the west, a small boat running for harbour over a ruffled sea, the race where two currents meet always kicking up a fuss, even on a calm day, and today it's beginning to rage. Nature's violence has never attracted Herman, he does not find it bracing. He shivers in his thin jacket, and goes down.

Bea rings the local electricity service. No reply. Saturday, of course. She pulls a face and tells Toby: 'why don't you go over to the Willings's?'

'The Willings have not been cut off.'

'It will be some muddle.'

'I don't know what I'll do with this casserole of Erin's. I suppose we could eat it cold.'

'I don't mind.'

'Erin's garlic casserole? *Cold*?'

'I don't mind if I go to the Willings's. Or not.'

Saying this, Toby realises it is true. Now he is old he is not so keen to test childhood heavens (perhaps because he needs them now more than he ever did; at the time he was in that magic world – playing with his young-looking mother, trailing around with Erin and her children, swimming, sailing, yelling with joy at the great Atlantic rollers, sailing alone for the first time out beyond the lighthouse – then, when Toby was inside the pages of a story-book heaven, he had had no idea he was there).

On the kitchen telephone Bea tries SeaLec which, unlike the local electrical service, is manned for emergencies twenty-four hours a day. The number's engaged. She puts down the receiver and dials again. Waiting for the call to be answered, she says over her shoulder: We might all go to the Willings's anyway.

'A piece of the island fell off,' says Erin, wide-eyed. 'I mean last winter when the snow melted it just came off and fell into the sea.'

Timbo has been dragged off to look at Merry's gerbil. Merry is the youngest Willings and adores Toby, who's remarkably patient with her. Bea worries a little sometimes that people will take advantage of Timbo's good nature. At first, it seemed touching and rather quaint, how her friends like Erin poured out their hearts to him; then, however little harm it seemed to do him, Bea was not sure she wanted her son exposed, at a time when he must be going through some disturbing changes himself, to so many sad worlds. (She believed – does believe – in the imprint theory. If a chimp can be brought up to believe it's a man, might Timbo emerge from childhood's chrysalis as a middle-aged woman with menstrual problems?)

Bea is honest, even ferocious with herself, and lately has acknowledged that when she imagines people taking advantage of Timbo, she means girls, females, young women. The girls, the mistresses or mates or whatever they call them nowadays, the daughter-in-law to come.

She will never intervene. She has made that vow. She will let him go to make his own mistakes. He may already have left.

It is evening. They are drinking at the Willings's, friends sitting round in a darkling room. The big picture-window gives on to the beach and the gale dashes against it. There are a lot of books, some pieces of good furniture, rather a muddle of tat and impulse and simply living. The books, of course, are mostly Merlyn's, a mixture of jacketless sober O.U.P., modern fiction and books about modern fiction (two of which are his own: *Bellow and After – The Horizontal Hero in Modern American Fiction* and *Journey into Inner Space, from Plath to Hawkes*). Much of the tat and some of the good stuff reflects

Erin's enthusiasms, which are passionate but ephemeral. So there are: a hooked rug the dog has chewed, some vertiginous muck-coloured pots and one rather satisfactory heavy blue dish, with the glaze hardly cracked, a crocheted rug, a rocker she re-caned, a jar of dusty dried grasses and a beautiful little painting of Merry propped up unframed on the shelf with the shells and pebbles and feathers and flowers and coronation mugs. On and off, between other crazes, Erin paints and Bea thinks she should do so more, she is happiest then. This one is ruralist school (though more Erin herself than any school): Merry at six or seven in a grubby blue smock, standing in the garden baleful with impatience to be out of the picture and off, clutching a kitten, a wreath of convolvulus in her tangled hair.

Bea peers more closely. 'That's lovely, Erin. It's one of the best you've done.'

Erin looks pleased but wistful. 'Oh, d'you think so.'

'Look, Herman. Isn't this beautiful.'

Herman comes over, glass in hand.

'You're a clever girl, Erin.'

Merlyn, who has been listening placidly enough to Vivaldi, his long denim legs crossed at the ankles, suddenly says: 'Erin, there isn't any ice.'

Erin blushes, she is at once confused and distressed.

Bea says: 'Oh, we're fine, we don't need ice.'

Merlyn is good-looking and he knows it. He has a noble brow. At the moment he is wearing a scowl and a frosty smile.

'On the contrary, sweet Beata, ice you shall have. Erin, shall you fetch the ice?'

Bea bites her lip.

Herman says: 'For God's sake, I'll fetch the ice.'

Bea thinks sometimes the only thing wrong with Erin is Merlyn. Then she thinks, but if Erin left Merlyn or Merlyn left Erin, might not Erin seek at once another Merlyn? Monsters attract victims and maybe victims need monsters. Anyhow, it is probably all more complicated than that. Other people's marriages are unfathomable. It could be I've got the whole thing inside out: Erin could have been unstable to begin with and without Merlyn snapping orders at her, she'd crack up. They could be right in bed, and Merlyn is good with the children, he's unguarded then, patient and gentle.

Whatever, he's being insufferable tonight. Merlyn and Herman are discussing stereophonics: the intellectual bourgeoisie's version of car-talk. Bea shivers. She's cold. Remembers the dead bird this afternoon, would be back in her little candled house.

'If I may, I'll just ring SeaLec again.'

'Could I ring SeaLec, Erin?'

The Willings too have a kitchen telephone, with a blackboard slate hung by it. Beside that there is a cracked Pears Soap repro mirror and a notice board covered with statements, signals and remarks from the three Willings children, Merry, Mercy and Tike. They are yellowing though. Mercy's pin-up of a punk rock star dates the nearly abandoned project, only Merry seems to use it now for tiny stick-men, stick-dogs, stick-cats, stick-worlds: a cosmos miniaturised somehow, but not yet domesticated, edgy still.

Erin is hacking at the ice, her eyes too bright.

'SeaLec night service is for emergencies only.'

'But we've no light, no heat.'

'Do you have a failure in your area?'

'I told you, we've been cut off.'

'Before we send an engineer would you please check that there is no failure in your area. If there is a failure in your area we will send a crew.'

'I-said-there-is-no-failure-our-supply-has-been-withdrawn.' Bea sighs. Losing one's temper rarely helps, she's discovered. Quite reasonably she says: 'I think there has been some muddle with the bill. I am asking you to re-connect us.'

'Please contact SeaLec in the morning.'

'But you *are* SeaLec.'

'This is an emergency service only, Madam.'

'And this is an emergency.'

This is how the world might end, she thinks: irreparable

disconnection. When she rings off the voice of electricity sounds wistful, almost human: 'If there is a failure in your area – '

They go on drinking with the Willings. Timbo comes in from his gerbil-visiting and Erin makes omelettes for them all (Tike's at camp and Mercy – oh, well, we don't talk about Mercy). Erin has checked the brimming tears with some fairly hefty pill, Bea guesses. She smiles and smiles and has drawn herself with shaky hand a new squashed strawberry mouth. Merry whines and fidgets (no child in this house is ever sent to bed), finally collapses in Merlyn's lap.

Bea knows she has drunk too much, they all have, though no one is drunk. She looks at Herman and thinks: how extraordinary, my husband: well, who is he? A man who sleeps in my bed and eats in my house, an intimate stranger. I know him very well and I have no idea of him at all.

They put on oilskins to walk the hundred yards along the beach. In the porch Erin pecks Herman and Bea on the cheek. You! she says, you're the happiest married couple round here.

Bea hugs Erin. Friends, she supposes, are family nowadays, which is why there's so much kissing. For whatever reason, we seem to feel the need to touch.

Timbo has gone ahead. Bea and Herman walk home through the wild night. There's the lighthouse but from the heaving of the sea you can catch only now and then the wink of the marker buoys; there may be a few mackerel boats out there but no fishing fleet any more. Lobster pots and mackerel. Jeannie Fisk, who has the big house on the promontory, American money and a taste for low lovers, told Erin who told Bea that mackerel are the souls of dead seamen which is why seamen's wives won't eat them (Jeannie should know: she has known enough seamen). Last summer Jeannie had a lobster party that was the talk of the coast, the poor, grey shelly creatures broiled alive before your eyes, blushing into death. But it was the mercury in them, or something: everyone got ill and a few nearly died. There was a run on Dr Collis Browne and for the rest of that summer no one bought lobster. Memories are short though.

'D'you remember Jeannie Fisk's lobster party?'

Herman groans.

Bea and Herman, stamping through the shingle in their oilskins, do not discuss the Willings. This is interesting, because they must both be concerned that their best friends' marriage appears to be on the rocks. Certainly it's deteriorated since the autumn. Irreparable disconnection, thinks Bea. And they were connected once – she does remember – just for a moment which seemed very long, like a slow-motion replay, there was a sexual, sensual connection between Erin and Merlyn that gave them both a kind of glory, the golden air of gods, discovered after a long row, just below the lighthouse, curled in the horseshoe cove not in flagrante but tasting the salt on each other's faces. That was before Mercy, before any of the children.

But it couldn't have been. We didn't know them then?

Of course! There are the children: Mercy, Timbo and Tike (Merry not yet born), very young, playing with sand in the other cove on the seaward side of the rocks. Came over in the Willings's big dory. Could have wandered into the sea, drowned in the rip-tide. While Merlyn and Erin enjoyed their sexy salt-lick. In our smaller dinghy we seemed to be approaching for hours and hours the curled couple on the hooped beach, from the distance one giant slumbering figure, then two interlocking androgynous shapes; finally the round of a breast and Merlyn's horseman head with those whorls of centaur-black hair spumed with grey (still the same ten, twelve years later: Grecian 2000? Merlyn? Never. Though he is vain, and that disarms a little, that he should be human).

Yet I wasn't angry or afraid, thinks Bea, pulling up the collar of her oilskin. Not that day. That was one of the good, gold days when beneath the watching lighthouse we sprawled and ate pink prawns and drank wine; the children played with the Willings's dog of the day and I crowned Herman with sea-vetch. Gathered sea-shells by the sea-shore.

One moment: Merlyn has his arm around Erin and passing the wine brushes my breast with his hand while I reach up for Timbo to take him from Herman.

Then at some point there is a very small accident. Timbo cuts his heel on a sharp razor-shell. He looks more surprised than alarmed at the blood and Herman carries him down to the dory. That was Timbo at four or five. It was nothing but the scar has grown with him.

.

Back in their dark house, illumined briefly every three minutes by the loom of the (automatic) lighthouse, the Tylers clamber out of their oilskins and hang them on the rack by the kitchen door. The Giacometti cat hurtles in past them in a fine rage, reduced by rain to bone and temper.

Timbo?

He must have gone up the outside steps to his room. Bea thinks of her son, lying in the dark. He never locks his door but since he was twelve or so Bea has always knocked before she goes in. Round about that age Timbo began to spend time in his room. He displayed a need for privacy which she appreciated and respected (though sometimes when he was neither playing records nor listening to the radio, Bea found herself – finds herself – listening to the silence from Timbo's room).

Herman's tired. He hadn't much wanted to go to the Willings's.

Candles. Under the stairs. Bea lights candles although they might as well go straight to bed. It's a housekeeping act: necessary to her. Should she call up to Timbo and offer him a candle?

At the kitchen table Bea huddles in her old Arran jacket and opens the mail they hadn't bothered with.

'D'you think Erin's on drugs?'

'Drugs?' Herman looks startled, as if Bea had suddenly

24

addressed him in operatic Italian. He's going to bed.

Bea opens the final demand on the electricity bill they paid last autumn, then the notice of disconnection.

She calls after Herman, going upstairs.

'We've been cut off.'

There's a gust outside. The candles gutter. The cat leaps from floor to chair and chair to table, finally settles on Bea's lap, its tail quivering with outrage at her cigarette smoke. Old witch and her mog, thinks Bea, in night kitchen. No spells though. Tonight it seems that there's not a spell left in the whole world.

Nevertheless.

2

'BEA TYLER! AND TIMBO, oh, my God, you're sexy. It can't be Timbo!'

'Hello, Jeannie.'

Ms Fisk encountered in the hypermarket appears un-touched by winter. Her skin's still the texture and colour of old boot, and she's wearing man's baggy trousers Katharine Hepburn might have thrown out, with the confidence of American women whose money – by the standards of that stripling country – is old. For reasons best known to herself she calls her husbands by their surnames: Fisk, Fantl, Froebl (as Jeannie points out, all effs). Not that she sees them, since she threw them all out long ago, and some died. Not that she murdered them, by lobsters or any other way: Jeannie was quite fond of them in her fashion, Froebl and Fantl and Fisk.

Jeannie is a phenomenon.

She might be a monster.

(There are so many scandals about Jeannie Fisk that Herman says if she did not exist it would have been necessary to invent her. There's probably no basis for the lesbian slander. That's just Jeannie's style: the way she swears like a cowboy, drinks like a man and enters a party as if she were kicking open the door of a western saloon. That woman would go with a goat, says Merlyn, who likes his females pliant and therefore dislikes Jeannie. She would too, if she fancied it, but Jeannie doesn't. Her tastes are insatiable and straight.)

At the crossroads between the freezer department and the canned food, stand Toby, Bea and Jeannie Fisk, Toby wishing that he had not streaked up to tower over his mother and meet Ms Fisk eyeball to eyeball; that he could still slip by unnoticed; that meeting Jeannie Fisk *anywhere* did not at once put you centre-stage.

'Is this really Timbo?'

Yes, this is Timbo.

With iron mildness, for she can be tough, Bea cuts off Jeannie's invitations, commands to drink, eat, swim in her ovoid pool dropped like a blue tear on the cliff-top. 'Sorry, Jeannie, got to stock the freezer – you know. Ring you?'

'That woman was ogling you,' says Bea to Toby when they're out of earshot, loading the trolley with superpacks of frozen food: chicken, turkey, fish, hamburgers, veg, strawberries, raspberries, loganberries, gallon drums of ice-cream –the sort of things she'd never buy at home, preferring when she can get it the modest fresh free-range: even the vegetarian towards which both she and Toby lately incline. But this is the coast, and holiday, and the tradition of holiday is to stock the freezer on the first shopping day.

Timbo remembers when he was nose-high to the freezer, what a magical place this used to be: a Brobdingnag land of giant foods for Titans. Now it seems simply gross, and in some way sad. Though he grins, he is not altogether happy, either, about his mother's remark. Wryly, he recognises that he has double standards: no prig, he simply doesn't like it when Bea says that sort of thing. From her mouth it sounds coarse.

(Bea has thought about this, about taboos, about the sexual element in the mother-son relationship. Had they been unnaturally close? You and Timbo – Jeannie Fisk said once – you're like an old married couple, hey Jocasta? Bea hasn't fretted – she's dry with herself. But she suspects she sometimes says the wrong thing, or at the wrong time.)

Mother and son, they step out into the blue, bright morning. The night's gale has washed the world and presented them with a spanking new day for the start of the season. All along the coast the summer people will be enacting the same rituals as the Tylers, taking down the storm shutters, stocking the deep-freeze; and the Tylers have been re-connected.

They load the van and Bea turns out of the car-park.

'Erin says Mercy's coming down today,' she says lightly, meaning nothing. 'She won't stay, I expect.' Mercy Willings has anorexia nervosa. Her condition is not mentioned and is widely discussed, especially at Jeannie Fisk's. 'It must be terrible for them. Dreadful for her too, of course. I wonder why she won't eat?'

Timbo looks out at the sparkling sea. On these Atlantic shores he can imagine ultima Thule, the edge of the world, the possibility of falling off.

'Because she doesn't want to, I suppose.'

As they take the turning on the coast-road there is a motor-bike coming towards them on the wrong side, having clipped the corner, the rider helmeted like an Eisenstein warrior, the sun dancing on his shaded visor. Even though collision is avoided Bea shakes as though she has been through a traffic accident. At that moment, when they nearly die and she survives and Toby too – like phantoms, it feels, in a shining world – Bea Tyler suspects that her husband is having an affair or he is going to die, or something of the sort is happening or will happen to one or another or all of them. There will be some catastrophe. One way or another, there will be a disconnection, this summer.

Bea tells Toby to say nothing to his father about the near-miss. After all, nothing happened, so there is nothing to tell. When they get home Toby is concerned for his mother, he feels, rather to his surprise, shaken himself, so it must be worse for her. Lately he has discovered that Bea, whom he always regarded as the strongest of the family, who quietly made the vital decisions for them all, who for so many years told Toby what to do (or more, helped Toby to find out what it was he wanted to do and then explained why it would or would not be practical to swop his Action Men for a kite, to learn to play the guitar, to sail alone to the lighthouse) – recently Toby has observed that this strong, virtuous, humorous, sharp-minded woman, his mother (well, of course she was virtuous, wasn't she?) will actually do as *he* says. Defer to him. It's an astonishing discovery. It gives him a power that is vaguely troubling. He doesn't much want to use it. He could send her to rest now but he won't.

So Bea says: 'Don't tell your father,' and they unload and they fill the freezer, labelling each package with date and contents. They have a picnic lunch on the porch of rolls and salami.

It's quite warm here. The cat deigns to sit on the mat. The famille Tyler converse. Bea says Erin hasn't said so but Bea knows Erin hopes they'll help with Mercy, though heaven knows what they can do. Herman says he might have to go up to town one day next week. Bea makes a funny story for Herman of the meeting with Jeannie Fisk, then the colour drains theatrically from her face and, not a crying woman, she bursts into tears, sitting there on the porch in the rocker.

Herman's really very sweet about it.

Bea Tyler never cries.

Lying on the bed in the hot, shaded room, Bea accepts Herman's brandy (probably quite wrong for shock) and is touched that he chafes her hands. She's icy, and the tears keep coming (I never cry). This has been a long marriage, it's quite famous. Her husband of twenty years is kissing her eyes, Herman is lying beside her, what follows will probably follow.

Their bodies are easy together, well acquainted, as is to be expected after so many years. Sometimes, indeed, as they writhe and coil so pleasantly, Bea has fancied they could leave their bodies to get on with it and go for a walk.

But then something unaccountable will happen. They will be astonished by a sudden prick of lust, a promise exchanged by the flick of an eye at a party; never before though, have they been caught out by failure.

They lie back, side by side, their eyes dry. Bea reaches for Herman's hand. Though he's thickened, her husband, he still has a young man's back, the cleft running down to youthful shanks and like hers his sandy hair shows little grey.

'We're all tired,' she says, but he's stricken. He lies in a theatrical posture, his arm across his eyes.

'What happened?' he says, 'what were you crying for?'

(A year ago Herman developed tachycardia. That is, his heart beat now and then abnormally fast: not in itself dangerous, though Herman was frightened and still expects, at any moment, the white horse of death to come a'galloping round the corner. His father died about the same time and Bea's mother. A health-freak at the office was felled by a stroke, playing squash. Jeannie Fisk had her breasts off. Herman's a bit of a hypochondriac, but still you could hardly blame him for suspecting that the Reaper might be around.)

'Oh, nothing. We just had a near-miss on the coast-road.'

Herman seems relieved, and she wonders why, what he was expecting her to say. He's cheerful, concerned ('my poor love'), keen to try again but though the juices flow briskly enough connection is not made.

Bea thinks: there is a failure in this area.

Bea thinks: Herman doesn't want to know about the near-miss. Quite suddenly she realises this, later that day, chopping tomatoes; her hand holding the Sabatier knife, halfway to the board, Bea understands that her husband is terrified of death.

When his father was dying and a death-watch had to be kept, Herman first had to go to Madrid (did he really have to go to Madrid?), then he, who had never had a serious illness in his life, contracted shingles (Bea remembers how patient he was with the shingles, almost as though he welcomed it) and no sooner had shingles quit the stage but there entered in a puff of smoke the demon tachycardia in the guise (spurious) of a heart attack. So it was Bea or Toby or Bea-and-Toby who saw the old man out (Toby was incredibly patient about that, would sit for hours in the fusty room reading S.F. while his grandfather choked and clicked and fidgeted and dozed and dribbled his way out of the world; did it damage Toby? Bea didn't know. She couldn't imagine them conversing but when Bea ran in, commuting from her mother's sick-bed, she

sometimes had the feeling that she had interrupted a conversation, which was absurd, because after the tracheotomy
her father-in-law could not speak).

Anyhow. The outrageous but possible thesis occurs to Bea,
she puts it to herself: that Herman could not make love to her
this afternoon because he sensed, even before she told him,
that she was contaminated by death, she had brushed against
those dark feathers and the dust was still on her.

Rather as the bereaved are so often shunned.

For her mother's funeral Herman had been in New York.

He had stood over his father's grave, ashy as a revenant
himself, as though he expected a long arm to reach out and
draw him in (or Lucifer Tachycardia himself to creep up and
tip him in from behind).

Bea is so stunned by this revelation the knife slips and she
cuts her hand. Nothing happens for a moment, then the
bright blood spurts out, all over the tomatoes. She crosses her
white kitchen and holds her hand under the cold tap.
One-armed, she presses kitchen paper to the wound, crosses
to the first aid box with the child-proof fastening (from the
days Toby might have knocked back the kaolin and morphine
diarrhoea mixture or Herman's sleeping pills or Bea's contra-
ceptive pills) but one-handed, for the blood has soaked the
kitchen paper and is spotting her skirt, Bea cannot open the
child-proof cupboard. Then the kitchen telephone rings.

'We had a fight last night.'

'Erin?' Perched on the high stool Bea is out of reach of the
kitchen paper, the telephone cord won't reach. In this state
Erin never announces herself or waits to hear to whom she is
speaking. She assumes it will be Bea and it usually is, though
even Toby in his time has had an earful. Bea remembers
Toby at seven when he was barely tall enough to reach the
wall telephone, standing twisting one foot quite expressionless
until apparently Erin paused and Toby said: Erin, I think you
want to talk to my mother.

'After you'd gone we had this terrible fight Bea I cried I
couldn't help it Bea and he struck me he's never done that
before I said Merlyn don't look at me like that don't look as if

31

you're going to strike me and he struck me he hit me Bea oh Bea every time I think of it I cry I can't stop crying I'm crying now Bea Bea it's so bad for Merry and Mercy's here Bea can I send Mercy over to you?'

'Erin, can you hold on a moment.'

'Oh Bea you don't know you and Herman you're so lucky I think and I think but if I left him he's so sweet to Merry you know how he is I'd be the wicked witch. Bea what shall I do if I could stop crying should I leave him Bea?'

'Erin, can you hold on a moment. I'm bleeding.'

Bea lays down the receiver very gently. It goes on talking. She has been sitting with one arm outstretched above waist level to avoid marking her skirt and to discourage the flow of blood, but the floor is spotted. She holds her hand briefly under the cold tap, snatches a drying up cloth and twists it tightly round the wound. Her hand has begun to throb and the tourniquet effect eases the pain. She feels a little dizzy with shock (shock upon shock today), lights a cigarette and in turning back to the telephone glances out at the beach where the tide is out and, on the sand revealed only at half-tide through the ebb, a company of dogs is playing. She looks at the telephone. The telephone is weeping. Leave it? Leave it and just walk out of the house?

Bea puts out the cigarette. With the thumb of the wounded hand she holds the cloth awkwardly in place. She needs the other hand for the telephone.

'Erin, listen. Where are the children now?'

'That's what I can't *bear* that they should suffer!'

'Erin, tell me. Is Mercy with you? Where's Merry?'

'Bea?' Erin is making an effort. It always comes round about now. The voice is still wobbly but the wailing ceases. 'Oh Bea I don't know what I'd do without you. Timbo and Herman too. All of you. Bless you all.'

'Erin, listen to me. D'you want us to have Mercy tonight?'

'Merlyn's got Merry. They've gone to fossil beach. He really is wonderful with Merry, Bea, she adores him, you know.'

Bea looks at the clock.

'Why don't you and Mercy come round here, Erin? About six? Mercy can stay if she likes.'

Well into stage three now, Erin is full of gratitude. Bea would rather she were full of joy, as she once was, as she remembers her sadly, as a girl.

Bea mops up the blood, paints the wound with iodine and Timbo gets her a plaster. They sit on the porch for a while.

Bea says: 'Gale warning at the Willings's again.'

Timbo pulls a face. He stretches on the swing seat as they watch the tide turn, the indigo water curl in reclaiming the sand that never quite dries out. The sky is wide and calm. Apart from gales, like last night's, reaching sometimes hurricane proportion, this is a coast known for its summers. Maybe the sea is poisoned, as they say, but it's hard to believe that now, it looks so mild. Oh, there are the dead and damaged birds, Jeannie Fisk's lobsters, the awful villas on the hinterland, those strange, wild-looking dogs, the motor cyclists; but at this tender dusky moment such horrors seem tales to frighten children. Timbo in the swing-seat, Bea in the worm-eaten rocker, Herman scraping the dinghy down by the breakwater.

'Those dogs,' says Bea.

She imagines that when the dogs depart the beach-bums arrive, if they are to be believed in, if they are not a figment of Erin's.

Timbo sees his father stand up stiffly, drop the scraper and clutch his back. He lopes into the kitchen for a beer and standing at the porch door snapping the tag off the can, his face and throat dry with salt already, Timbo sees his mother – that injured and virtuous woman – patiently rocking as if rocking would get her anywhere. Just lately his parents seem to have become incompetent and this touches and troubles him a little. One day he may feel something stronger: contempt or anguish, though anguish is more likely. Before something happens, Timbo wonders if he should get a divorce from his parents.

The telephone rings. Bea jumps. Timbo goes to answer it.

'The Catarullas. They couldn't find the key. I told them under the doormat.'

Bea thinks of these strangers in her house.

'What did they sound like?'

'People.'

'Perhaps Americans don't have doormats.'

Timbo says: 'Who's giving the parties this year?'

'Lord, the parties.' Bea catches sight of Erin making her way across the shingle with her daughter, two figures that seem to be approaching from a great distance like moon-walkers. 'Us, I suppose. And Jeannie Fisk and the Willings.' She catches her son's hand as he passes. 'What would happen, d'you think, if we didn't give a party?'

'You'd be ostracised, cast out. They'd tar and feather you.'

Bea smiles at her tall, salt-faced son.

'Obligations,' she says and enjoys the word. 'One has ob-li-gations. And here come two of them.'

Here's Erin, fine after the afternoon's storm. That's how it sometimes takes her after tears (this confuses her friends who, having been cheerful, fall into despondency for Erin, only to find that she has forgotten all about it); or perhaps Erin is trying for Mercy's sake. Either way, she has scrubbed her face and is wearing a long clean paisley skirt and peasant blouse laced lopsidedly down the front; also, she sports wooden-soled exercise sandals and a granny shawl. Beside her mother's soft bulk, Mercy is a skinny phantom: poor tormented soul, pale ghost she seems, who has arrived perhaps on the wrong planet. That's what Bea thinks. Jeannie Fisk says she's a pain in the neck and you can see her point of view, too.

Mercy's shoeless. She has sand between her toes, she has starved ankles and through walking barefoot her heels have built up a thick cutaneous layer as tough almost as horn. Pumice-stone won't touch it. Once Mercy walked all day with a thorn in her heel and never noticed. Her wrists too are brittle, thin as baby bangles, and Bea knows that beneath the jeans her legs are the same. She's had treatment, but it didn't work. Eating just enough, Mercy is not dying, but the condition makes her abnormally susceptible to dangerous ailments – she had double pneumonia last winter.

'What a wonderful night,' said Erin, too brightly. 'Isn't it beautiful. You summer people get a better sunset – we're sideways on. Oh, God, no, Timbo, I'd better not drink or I'll howl,' she says, taking the drink and ruffling Toby's hair. Toby grins. Bea thinks: children, children, how strange – Timbo allows Erin liberties I haven't dared to take for two or three years at least. I don't fret. He's a loving son. Jeannie Fisk's an idiot with her taboos – she's borne no children.

Herman's left his scraping and gone off somewhere. Bea puts Erin's garlic casserole in the oven. Mercy and Toby drift down the beach, leaving the women on the porch.

Bea says: 'Can't you find someone for Mercy?'

'Bea, love, you know, I'm an *academic* psychologist. They don't let us loose on patients. We can't see the trees for the wood. Clinicians despise us: well, you can't blame them really – up to their arms all day in other people's dirty washing.' Erin's ample hair is falling down already; Bea has a vision of her friend as a mad old woman with wild grey hair, keening at her door on a stormy night. 'Well, there's this Bonstock man – you know, *The Family is Sick* – treats the whole mare's nest.' Erin hoots. 'Can't you imagine Merlyn submitting himself to that!'

'Well, if it would really help Mercy.'

Erin takes a slug of her drink and her eyes brim: 'Oh, Bea, am I wicked? Sometimes I feel such a wicked woman. I think what we're doing to the children and sometimes I think I want to kill him, I really want to kill him and I imagine it, all kinds of terrible ways.'

'Erin – '

'And then I see you, this life, so orderly, so beautiful, lovely Timbo. I can't even *cook*! I kill everything with garlic and I always mean not to and I always do it.'

'You could stop buying it.'

'But I can't! I CAN'T STOP BUYING GARLIC!'

Bea's hand throbs, Erin is talking crazily, but it is true – at least, it has been true – there is peace here, this place has always worked for her. Momentarily she closes her eyes, in petition, if she had been a praying woman, and opens them to find that it has worked, once again – even Erin is silenced by a certain stillness that comes sometimes around dusk, a quality in the air and the dying light that compels silence. Two shapes, from here hermaphrodite, Toby and Mercy are making their way back to the house.

'Look' breathes Bea and Erin nods. The two women smile at each other. They are old friends. That's a tough weed, friendship. The light and the warmth drain from the land and the dogs depart. Now come the Honda warriors screaming up the coast road. And the beach-bums move in, in Bea's imagination, her seeing eye, to occupy the empty sand. She shivers and says: 'Come on, let's go in.'

They eat (or rather the others eat and Mercy plays with a roll and a lettuce leaf) in the kitchen, Bea and Erin and Mercy and Timbo.

Erin mostly talks. A dull, purple stain has come up on her cheek and her mouth is slightly swollen, so Merlyn really did hit her. Erin and Bea mostly talk about the three parties that will, as always, mark the season. Mercy is protective of her mother – she always has been – and Bea wonders what hell she is going through now. Bea and Mercy have always got on. Mercy used to love helping with the birds when Bea had a patient. Bea has tried to talk to her about this starving business, and Mercy listened her out, but all she would say was: 'I just don't like eating animals.' 'Well, that's fine,' said Bea, 'a vegetarian diet's very healthy. I've practically given up meat myself.' Then from Mercy there would be that maddening, heartbreaking litle shrug, dip of the shoulders, that drove Bea finally, in the hospital room, to take Mercy's hands and say: 'Mercy, you must eat or you will die.' Then Mercy said: 'But you see, I can't swallow.'

Mercy will eat only for Timbo. Bea has just noticed this, and wonders what to make of it.

Erin says: 'Honestly Bea, I'm not sure I can stand Jeannie Fisk's party this year.'

Timbo says something to Mercy and the girl pulls off another little corner of bread and nibbles it. Five minutes ago they were children, coevals who had scrapped and played all their lives, summer after summer; when they were about thirteen there was an estrangement; now they could be lovers. Timbo could be making love to Mercy.

'Oh, mother, you know quite well you'll go,' says Mercy, and it's true, Erin always does go to the parties, nothing would keep her away, in manic or depressive phase, in sickness or in health, once with a broken leg, once with Merry's mumps. Bea thinks she understands and finds Erin's motive touching – people have all kinds of reasons for going to parties but rare is the one of their age, the middle age, who goes as hopefully as Erin. Erin believes, as once we all did, in the accessibility of joy through encounter. Erin believes in Happiness and Virtue and perhaps it is no odder that she should expect to come across these good souls at some bash of Jeannie Fisk's, than that Christ should be discovered in the company of thieves.

The casserole is appalling. It occurs to Bea that Erin uses so much garlic to keep the devil away. Certainly no fiend in his right mind would sup from Erin's spoon.

Erin and Bea take their coffee into the sitting-room while Timbo and Mercy wash up. Or Timbo washes and Mercy perches on the high stool, smoking. Or they wash up quickly and go and flop on the porch.

'It's pretty awful,' says Mercy. She has long hazy hair that clouds her face. 'But how can I leave her like this?'

Timbo nods. 'They've got to manage by themselves some-time.'

In the sitting-room Bea and Erin sit by the light of the big paper pumpkin lamp, slung low over the coffee-table.

'Such a pretty room' sighs Erin as she often has before, 'you're so lucky Bea,' as though some good fairy had visited Bea and bestowed upon her the sanded floor, the two glowing rugs, the Victorian chair, the Thonet rocket, the grandmother clock, the honeysuckle curtains, the calm bookshelves, the Staffordshire dogs, the sepia prints of famous wrecks along this dangerous coast.

Bea does not tell her friend about the near-miss. Nor does she ask Erin to stay the night. She cannot really believe that Merlyn will be waiting out there on the dark beach with an axe, though one day he may be.

Jeannie Fisk has a gun, everyone knows that.

The world is full of killing weapons: you could kill yourself chopping tomatoes. Knives and guns and stones. Lobsters kill too. When he was small Timbo cut his heel on a razor-shell.

Bea unravels the knitting wool the terrible cat has tangled. It's the colour of sticks and stones, but soft. Worthy, the Willings's old dog, has tachycardia, Erin tells Bea, just like Herman. Actually, Erin says the vet says, it could be cardiac neurosis: that is, Worthy thinks he has heart disease so he imitates the symptoms. Who would have suspected that famous rug-eater of such guile? Suddenly, the whole thing seems so absurd they both laugh, the two women, not at men or dogs but everything, the whole idiot caper.

Mercy and Timbo come in and don't know what the joke is, which sets the women off again.

'You're so good for me, Bea,' says Erin, mopping her eyes, and Bea wonders, not for the first time, at Erin's powers of recuperation.

'You'll be all right?'

They'll be fine, because Timbo walks them home along the beach and there's no axe-man waiting. Just some bums or hippies or freaks or children, sleeping on the shingle above high-water mark under the soft night, forgetfulness for blankets and for pillows, stones.

3

THE SUMMER SEASON is divided into three parties.

When they were all young, before Jeannie Fisk arrived with her money, before any of them had money, the social life on this strip of the coast was hardly structured at all. Most were starting families so in the afternoons the women, pregnant or skirted by toddlers, infants slung on the hip or in Indian back-packs, drifted down to the beach and spent an hour or two gossiping and dozing, exchanging the small change of maternity or talking sometimes about books or reviews of books gobbled in the exhausted hour of peace when the last child had been tucked away. While the men would make storm shutters for their houses or sailing dinghies from kits or sweat it out on the train from the city (no six-week vacations then). Though it could not have lasted more than a few years, this time seemed to Bea to have gone on through a whole decade of sunshine and pleasant fatigue, sand trailed in and out of the house, geraniums wilting on the porch, naked children in the sun, small dramas. Bea had her miscarriages. Francine Fox had post-natal depression and hallucinated that lobsters were following her to eat her brain. (She's better now but still has an allergy to crustaceans.) One couple, long gone, were immolated in their shanty beach-house that had been a fisherman's hut when fish were fish (the girl had cried I'll burn the bastard burn him).

Then in the evenings – usually weekends, Saturday night – there were informal ceremonies of innocence. Someone would call out come over later, and any time after seven they would meet on one of the half-built porches, drink beer from cans or cheap wine, eat salad, or sausages fried on a boy-scout fire until Harry Fox constructed the first barbecue." No one changed, several brought their children in carry-cots or left them with the Willings's au pair, but mostly they brought them. A little pot was smoked, then it became legal and no one bothered except Francine when she had trouble with lobsters. Possibly, as Jeannie Fisk would put it, there were those who coveted their neighbour's wife's ass but if there was any of that it went unconsummated, Bea guessed. They lived – like the Bryozoans, the fossils of the moss-like colonial animals in which she had lately taken an interest – as zooecium dwellers in a zoarium, the good of each individual in harmony with the well-being of the whole.

Perhaps because this may be their last summer together Bea has recently thought a lot about that time. It seems (like her beloved fossils) both petrified and accessible. So she can see Erin when she was lovely and it was still good with Merlyn, reaching up from the lilo to brush the sand from Mercy's shoulders, the sand running down between her own breasts as Mercy wriggles then Erin hugs her daughter and draws her down, Mercy squealing with delight until Erin draws her down and she has captured her rapturous daughter. And furry downy Erin with the sand prickling her heavy breasts is always reaching for Mercy and Mercy tumbling out of the white sky: thus they would be caught, these children of Pompeii, in the killing preserving larva. (Trace fossils give indirect evidence of life in the past, footprints for instance, burrows, borings.)

Then she remembers Erin crouched on her haunches crying because Mercy or Tike has fallen and cut a leg while the Belgian au pair was sulking over the cooking sherry and Erin and Bea – wicked pair of wanton sluts – were playing hookey in a boutique in town. Erin crying sets the child crying too though the graze hardly hurts at all and Timbo, a grave seven, watches, slightly shocked, like a virgin at an orgy.

Timbo himself will be cut with a razor-shell and Bea sees how patiently the normally undextrous Herman kneels to bind the wound with a clean handkerchief dipped in sea water, talking all the time to the boy, then he carried him down to the dory.

That came first though. Timbo was four or five then.

I'll burn the bastard burn him cries the girl running down the beach in a blood-coloured shift, her hair Medusa-spiked, but she was never really one of them. Though they were ashamed afterwards; especially Francine Fox who has seen ultima Thule herself and nearly fell right off (a lobster pushed her).

On the whole we got on very well, we Ammonites and Belemnites: extinct Cephalopods.

After Jeannie Fisk came, belting round the point in her Range Rover, the summers changed. They would have changed anyway. There was more money, the houses were pretty well finished and furnished, the children could go off on their own (though there were worries about the coast-road which, round about that time, ten years or so ago, became both noisier and busier – Tike had a narrow escape there: he was thrown free but his bicycle was mangled).

The quality of the wine improved, spirits were drunk more often, the men worked harder to counterbalance their longer vacations, Erin (this was before Merry) astonished everyone by going back to work, the home-made sailing dinghies were passed on to the children or scrapped or sold and replaced with dashing class racers that on a bright summer afternoon in the bay tacked and gybed like pilot fish round Jeannie Fisk's motor-yacht (Jeannie catches fishermen; also tope and lately a couple of the shark that used to bask, pondering plankton, well off-shore, but in the last few seasons have moved in, alarming swimmers. It is a sight to see Jeannie braced to use the gaffe, swearing like a pirate. Anything under six feet she throws back, though her salty lovers can be any size at all).

There would still be evenings on the porches, but they got a little wilder.

How far anyone went, Bea was never sure but she would not have been surprised.

Except for the taboo. They were family. But perhaps that was an extra kick? Incest.

Jeannie Fisk swore she'd seen Francine Fox and Merlyn going at it, hammer and anvil, on fossil beach. But wickedness too can be in the eye of the beholder.

So when Jeannie arrived they were ripe.

Before they even saw her they were aware (gossip, lights at night on the promontory) that the empty crazy villa on the cliff-top was occupied. Because of the watch-tower on the cliff-edge, the green leaded domes, the minaret, the grandiose scale of the enterprise, they'd long ago christened it variously Xanadu, Rosebud's palace, the Gatsby place. It had been empty for twenty years and once, when Bea trespassed with Timbo and Tike the boys had found a spotted toad alive in the leaves in the drained swimming-pool, Bea was surprised in the conservatory among the damply dead exotica by the flash of some small and brilliant yellow bird that must have been nesting in the vine. Then Francine rang Erin who told Bea that some billionairess, a Deterding or an illegitimate daughter of Howard Hughes or scion of Getty, had snapped it up unseen and was living there on bourbon and dried curry. Expecting something like a menopausal Patti Hearst, they were startled therefore when Hepburn straight out of *The African Queen* arrived on the Foxes' porch in fourth gear, dumped her Ranger on the shingle and announced: 'I'm Jeannie Fisk. I've bought that goddam cliff.'

'You remember that first party?' Bea lies on the lounger by Jeannie's pool, sipping lime juice spiked with something. Jeannie grunts, flat on her back dressed as a salad with cucumber on her eyes. Far below, out in the bay, a little

42

yacht seems becalmed on a brazen sea: Timbo and Mercy? Jeannie wears plastic-rimmed Mickey Mouse sunglasses and a green eye-shade. You wouldn't imagine her to be a woman who fussed about her looks and her efforts at beautification are spasmodic and ironic. Fuckit she says, throws off the salad and dives into the pool, churning up and down like a cheerful brown dog. Bea smiles and yawns, blinks at the violent light that kills even colour, and pulls down the brim of her big sun-hat: it's straw, and dapples the sun like water. Of all the community, Bea – fastidious, a little dry, contained – might have been expected to find Jeannie appalling, and so she does. And yet Bea thinks sometimes that Jeannie is the only person (the only woman?) round here she can stand, because only Jeannie never asks anything of her. (Even when she had her breasts off a year ago.) Bea slips up here sometimes for a holiday, half an hour off duty. Affection? Possibly. Certainly Jeannie Fisk has a courage, a spirit, she admires and envies. If Bea were really in trouble it is possible that she might turn to Jeannie. In literature the American woman would be dreadful; life is more complicated than that, thank God, thinks Bea as Jeannie rejoins her and stands towelling herself down, shaking off bright drops of water. (At the edge of the bikini top there's the tiniest puckering of the skin, no more. Jeannie doesn't wear padded bras to make up for her loss, that wouldn't be her style.)

There's a bite of rosemary and verbena in the air, and some more languorous, visceral scent, as of those curiously dangerous plants in the ruined conservatory: flesh-like, decaying.

'You remember at your first party,' Bea says. Jeannie snorts.

'Christ. Francine Fox stripped off.' Jeannie doesn't oil herself. She lights a menthol cigarette.

'We weren't used to that sort of high life. We were very simple. Some of us still are.' Bea's tone is light but she means what she says.

'You're solid gold, Bea. Incorruptible.'

'Oh, sometimes I wouldn't mind being corrupted.'

'You let them use you.'

Bea squints into the sun: on the boat out there the sun has sparked a piece of glass, a bottle or a mirror or Mercy's reflecting sunglasses that give you back your own face and tell nothing. Apart from this one piercing jewel, the sea is now the colour of watered Pernod, that's the light.

The light on this coast is cruel and curious, nothing escapes it.

'Isn't everyone used?' Except Jeannie, thinks Bea.

'Women,' says Jeannie. 'By men, children, parents, dogs.'

It is possible to see how to someone of Jeannie's un-complicated vision Bea Tyler might appear a passive acceptor of roles. Though if she were so, there would not be the odd accord between the two women. Bea has had this tussle with Jeannie before and feels sorry for Froebl, Fantl and Fisk, though their crimes may have been terrible and they may have asked Jeannie to wash their underpants. Probably not. With Jeannie's money there is always someone to wash underpants. Jeannie has probably never heard of underpants. That's money.

(On her solitary expeditions among the rock-pools, barefoot in faded jeans, Bea thinks sometimes that it would be convenient to believe in God. It seems more likely however that if some omniscient consciousness orders and disorders their lives, it might be a novelist. Only a maker of fiction, it seems to her, could have set them all down in this searching light, implied a shape, a destiny – and then forsaken them so abruptly when invention ran out. Or is he/she planning a showdown?)

Money gives Jeannie Fisk the sheen of film stars or royalty encountered in the flesh, of beautiful women, powerful men and sexually magnificently adjusted couples. Some of Herman's business contacts are like that: dreary drip-dry men perpetually in transit via the Hiltons of the world, yet they have something, that gloss of power, or of money, the coinage of power. Bea is not impressed by it but it interests her.

At that first party Jeannie wore one of her caftans from Arabia – gold thread on peacock silk – as if it were a cheese-cloth sack she'd pulled on after swimming. ('Paris?' hissed Francine Fox, who was always stunning herself, malgré lobsters. 'From a Persian market,' said Bea, 'she sleeps in them.')

Actually, Jeannie sleeps raw summer and winter, she told Bea once and Bea imagines her under her goose-down duvet, breastless as an Amazon waiting for the fisherman to come in; and if the sailor never came home from the sea Jeannie would just shrug and turn over. Francine Fox stripped off at that first party. She had been taking something to keep the lobsters at bay that did not mix with gin, or mixed too well; then there was the heat and the atmosphere of Xanadu, the mad architecture, Jeannie's trompe-l'oeil interior décor, the scent of dead or dying succulents. Whatever. Francine, who had always been lovely, a lovely girl, black hair very soft, most beautiful breasts, a living picture of the pliant female, stood poised on the first diving board and unzipped.

Fell.

Francine is always falling from the diving board.

Bea always thinks of her falling.

Everything is shattered by the light. Bea is wrong about Jeannie: she has borne one child. She has, now Bea comes to notice, a Caesarian scar to prove it.

The refracted light from the white slabs round the pool is too much: later this season Jeannie will have them torn up and replaced with a pink stone the colour of milky quartz.

They are talking about children; Jeannie had one son by Froebl or Fantl, that would be twenty or twenty-five years ago and she hasn't seen him for fifteen years ever since she sacked Fantl or Froebl.

'You don't miss him?'

'I never knew him, so what could I miss? The idea of him,

45

maybe?' Jeannie makes a rare confession: 'I was going to meet him once. I got on a plane and I got off. I never arrived. I thought I'm not getting in that tangle. My idea of him, his idea of me – we never stood a chance. His name was Peregrine – for God's sake, *Peregrine*.'

'Where is he now?'

'Some beach.' Jeannie grins. 'His father put him through Ivy League, all that, and one day he just walked off to Katmandu or wherever.'

'You do think of him.'

'I wish him luck. You know, I write him sometimes but I never mail the letters. It used to worry me, that I'd die alone. But I'm not like you Bea – one of nature's mothers.'

Bea looks down at her green drink. 'I'm not sure, Jeannie, what I am.'

Gastropods, she thinks, I love them, Bellerophon and Hippochrenes for their names, and elusive Aporrhais.

The Willings will give the first party of the season if Merlyn does not take an axe to Erin or Erin does not crack up or Mercy does not submit to anorexia or Worthy to cardiac neurosis.

Wistfully in keeping with her bountiful image, Erin always lays on mountains of food. Saffron rice with garlic, turkey with garlic, chicken with garlic, garlic vol-au-vents, lettuce with garlic, garlic bread.

'Garlic fishballs,' says Bea, remembering the year before last.

'Garlic sausages,' groans Herman. Bea thinks he still hasn't relaxed. He's caught a tan already but his face is strained and there are dark hollows beneath his eyes. Normally he seems younger than he is, but sometimes lately he has taken on the look of his father.

Husky, dusky, sexy, waif-like Francine has called to borrow spaghetti and stayed to yawn and sip mint tea on the porch.

'Lobster with garlic!' she suggests and they play the game, keep the ball going, egging each other on like children, tears in their eyes, until like children they are shamed. They've been caught out by Timbo who's come up the beach to ask if he can take the lugger. He looks at them. He doesn't judge them. So dispassionate he appears, an old man of charity and silence, her son, barefoot in bleached trunks, asking for the lugger as politely as a stranger, though he knows he can take it any time. Erin said once, halfway in her cups, what's the matter with them, Bea? We weren't like that? We had causes. Why don't they go out and protest?

'Because there's nothing to protest about, I suppose.'

'Bea – with the world as it is?'

'That's the point. There's too much. The revolution's over, Erin. It didn't happen.'

'Well, at least you don't have to worry about Timbo.'

It is true that Erin has to worry about Mercy. And it is true that a good preventative for anorexia or any other form of suicide is to heave up paving-stones in Paris round about '68 (ancient history), or kidnap an industrialist or hi-jack a plane or gun down a president. Indeed such things, or similar things, still happen and might be enough to give Mercy back her appetite, but this is a different revolution that makes Paris look like childhood. Now the industrialist is always found tortured or clubbed or cut or shot to death in the boot of a car or a street or a ditch (or once tried and buried in Holland, with headstone); and missing heiresses do not survive terrorist bivouacs.

The Willings's party is always given when the season is still fresh. It's hot but the leaves are spanking green on the trees and the collared turtle doves explain coo-koo-coo. Apart from Jeannie's steaming horticultural fantasy, the Willings are the only family to have a proper garden because they are year-round people. Like the house, it's charming and dis-ordered: at this time of year a hot wind comes up about 4 o'clock and drifts of blossom fall from the neglected quince and apple and pear and cherry. There is the memory of a herbaceous border (a mad project in this climate) but geraniums, and later in the season marigolds and nasturtium will flourish among the dust and bindweed and convolvulus. The herbs survive too, remarkably resilient to the wild and bitter winters, so as you walk your feet press a sweet sharpness. Oddly, Erin has never planted garlic – like an alcoholic who doesn't keep drink in the house.

'Are you staying for the party?' Timbo asks Mercy. The lugger gybes and Mercy ducks. The wind's falling light. Mercy leans back, trailing her hand in the water. Timbo thinks how fragile her limbs are, like bones emptied of marrow. Except accidentally, they have not touched, they are still not sure of each other though they look the most composed young people. Timbo realises that once they touch, all will change and he's not sure yet if he's ready. Mercy wears those reflecting sunglasses, she looks up at Jeannie Fisk's house on the promontory and the windows flash like a palace of crystal. Mercy thinks V. Woolf has something like that, hasn't she: lighthouses and headlands talking in pure light? When she's well enough Mercy attends English seminars. She doubts if she has the correct attitude; all those old writers preoccupy her as personal acquaintances (and their characters), so V. Woolf with her horse-beautiful face is an ever-present phantasm; and she has travelled with Zelda.

Mercy will stay for the party because, as she says, her parents may otherwise kill one another.

'Have you noticed,' says Bea, driving to market with her friend Erin in the estate van, 'none of us has parents?'

It is an anthropological study to watch the consumers raiding the hypermarket. It's a dreadful place, you could lose your soul here, crack up (Francine Fox, in her crustacean period, was found weeping among the frozen meats: she hardly made sense at all for a week). But since most of the summer people have freezers and children, and everything is cheaper there, of course, they all go. They go for courage in couples or, if alone, greet each other like shades in limbo, poor lost bowed creatures trundling their trollies across acres, shuffling to queue at the pay-outs where the attendants – pale and tongueless indeed as Charon's assistants – take their dues and they are at last released out into the bright air.

'They've moved the knickers' yells Erin above the musack. This week's loss-leader is dog food. Lucky Worthy.

Erin's face is still bruised. She is stocking up for her party as though the end of the world may be next week. Bea watches in wonder as Erin buys: 6 lb frozen mince, 10 lb frozen tuna, two frozen turkeys, one gammon leg, four frozen ratatouilles, twelve packs dried Chinese, sixteen packs boil-in-the-bag rice, twenty-five frozen vol-au-vent cases, ten packets of genuine Italian spaghetti, fifteen bottles mouth-raking red plonk, ten French loaves, two dozen green peppers, two dozen chilli. No spirits: the Willings are the least well off of the beach people; it's surprising, in fact, they can afford all this (they can't – after the party Erin will scrape the plates and re-freeze the detritus for risotto). At the veg stack Erin pauses and looks pleadingly at Bea, who shakes her head. No, not garlic. Though Bea knows quite well that once her back is turned Erin will sneak back and stock up.

'This place,' cries Erin, 'this place always makes me buy too much.' Distraught, she looks at her heaped trolley. It's true. From the moment you enter the portals everything conspires to steal your will, your identity even. When you come to add it up, what with the petrol, there's not much saved. Yet still they all go. There's Francine Fox in hot pants and a pink halter top buying Edam and vodka pretending she hasn't seen them, which is not like Francine. (Bea knows that from here Francine will drive twenty miles down the coast, then twenty miles inland to buy vodka. Lovely sexy Francine is a closet alcoholic. Only Bea knows this for certain because Francine told her: that Harry gives her a dress allowance she spends on vodka. Bea would probably have found out anyway, because people tell her that sort of thing. As it happened, Bea had the little Foxes one afternoon two summers ago and delivered them back to find Francine throwing up on the sofa.

Bea sent the children next door to the Willings, cleaned up the sofa, made black coffee in Francine's kitchen, checked Francine had not taken drugs, and sat reading Harry's *New Technology* and smoking and feeling sad, while Francine snored on the sofa, then woke up.

Francine talked a lot of nonsense and some truth: the wise foolishness of the invalid drunk. And Bea listened and listened to Francine's wild and wonderful tale, of which she believed slightly less than half. What Harry, that practical, wholesome, hairless fellow did or did not do in bed. How Francine blamed herself. How she was not going to blame herself any longer. At last, panting, Francine ran out of stories. Then Harry came in and he had neither horns nor a tail.

In bed that night Bea did say something to Herman.

'So what did you tell her to do?'

'Well, nothing. How could I? I don't know what she should do.'

Herman grumbled: 'What's the point then? What do you do?'

'I witness. That's all.')

If there is a secret novelist at work and all these souls are figments, Bea has enough information to be the author. But she is not an instigator, and her charity is at least as congenital as her dryness.

Bea and Erin hump the bags to the wagon. In spite of everything, Erin is in good spirits because there is going to be a party. She smiles upon the world, this bruised, large, middle-aged woman in a little girl's print dress. The windows are down, the sun is shining, the coast-road is clear and Erin really believes, Bea, that this is the summer Mercy will get better.

(Past the point of the near-miss Bea breathes more evenly. And there is something very touching about Erin.)

50

'She's staying for the party,' says Erin. 'That's a good sign, isn't it?'

Bea smiles.

The wind has whipped the pins from Erin's hair. She looks like an ageing Rhine maiden, her hair streaming behind her. As they gallop along the coast-road they spill Erin's pins by the wayside into the dry grass, the struggling tamarisk, the wild stunted herbs that fringe the hinterland.

Suddenly they don't want to go home yet. There's no need. Merlyn can look after Merry and Timbo and Mercy can look after themselves (or Timbo can look after Mercy). Halfway home there's a beach-bar in the middle of nowhere – a bamboo shack really, with a few metal tables on the sand, Martini umbrellas and a counter that sells drink, pizzas and dusty aerosols of sun-oil. One of the more energetic beach-bums runs it. He wears faded trunks and that's all, and since hardly anyone ever comes here he smokes pot in the sun and perfects his tan and dreams of . . . Well, what does he dream of? Nothing. Everything. Who knows, since he rarely speaks, and then faintly, though he has a lovely smile.

Timbo, thinks Bea, will this be Timbo? Perhaps it will. Oddly, I shan't mind too much.

Worthy, who has been grinning in the back seat, follows them down the beach with an old man's, bow-legged gait, collapses gratefully in the shadiest corner of the rattan awning that flaps in the hot breeze. The boy brings him water and he wags, but the effort of rising to drink it is too much. The boy brings Bea and Erin the bar's speciality, a long pretty drink crackling with ice and spliced with white rum: it's called an ice-cracker and it's either that or Coke or Coke or that – the bar's range is limited and strangers who complain are regarded by the locals with gentle scorn. Not that many strangers come here anyway: it looks a dump.

'Nnn.' Erin shakes off her exercise sandals and wiggles her toes. 'Joe, that is heaven.' The boy smiles his lovely smile and brings them a plate of the fat pink prawns he reserves for regulars; they've come out of the primitive ice-box where he stores the pizza and coke, and have a light coating of frost.

Good dog Worthy has recovered enough to stagger to the water-bowl, he laps and flops down again, legs stuck out straight. It's mid-day. The rattan ceases to flap, falls still, the stilled sea takes on the dream-light of an hallucination.

'It could be a mirage,' says Bea. 'Look, the island's gone. Sometimes this place is all light.'

'You know past-life therapy,' says Erin.

'Not first-hand.' Bea has suspected that Erin is hatching something. 'Reincarnation?'

'More or less. Well you see, Bea, the point is we've all lived one or more lives before.' Erin's eyes shine with evangelist fervour or possibly with Joe's special ice-cracker. 'And we've been hurt. Well not necessarily *us* but some ancestor perhaps, and we still feel the pain. It just goes on and on.'

'I thought it was discredited?'

'Oh, you know what prigs they are. Poor Binder was nearly stoned when he did the first paper, but it's not the first time flat-earthers have had to adjust their perspective. What it amounts to is, Mercy could be ill because God knows when – in the potato famine, in some war, some pogrom – someone starved to death. It could equally be someone shot in the leg at Waterloo, then she'd limp. You see? Mercy pays.'

'Nice work for genealogists.'

Yet Bea could see it: it was possible, really possible in a way not quite dotty. No madder than her passion for fossils. To believe that the past is ever present, there is no jam today. The past rules, we are all trace fossils, evidence of life that has been.

Bea squints at the sun. No, surely we qualify, adjust, are capable of our own determinations. Never mind, let Erin dream if it helps.

There's Joe, slumped in the sun whittling a stick.

The women yawn with heat and rum, smile.

'It's good to do this,' says Bea. 'Let's forget we have children?'

Erin giggles. 'We're two rich ladies looking for gigolos.'

'Marienbad.'

'The film or the place?'

'God, that was donkey's years ago.'

Suddenly Erin lets out a deep breath. She looks very young at this moment to Bea, but then one's friends never age till they die.

'Oh Bea, I wish!'

Erin and her inexpressible longings: that's one of her most disarming qualities (unless, like Jeannie, you happen to find it irritating: she's a good kid says Jeannie – who is a jam today person – but it's time she realised now is all we have).

'We were young?' wonders Bea, but Erin grins and shakes her head, meaning I don't know what I wish.

For all her banshee wailing there is something rapturous about Erin's approach to life. Every experience is so urgent and intense. Finding she was pregnant, for instance, when she was forty-two and had gone back to work and her marriage was already rocky. There'd been a gale of weeping, of course, when she first confessed to Bea. Jeannie had brusquely counselled abortion, Francine hadn't helped by wordlessly hugging Erin, her eyes brimming with sisterly tears. Then, just as everyone had begun to fear for her always precarious balance, Erin had suddenly joyously embraced her condition, appearing at a party of Jeannie's in cheesecloth maternity fig long before anything showed, revelling, it seemed, in this hormonal Indian summer, burbling of babies. And then Merry had been born and breast-fed for a year (even when Erin had gone back to work, in the senior common room, shamelessly at seminars).

Somehow they had all been touched by Merry's birth, even those who disapproved.

Perhaps it made them feel they weren't so old, so fearful. Merry's had been an easy delivery and she was a pretty child. Merlyn stole her, once she'd been house-trained and learned to eat with a spoon.

But the two women are on a spree, they have agreed to forget children.

'You and Herman,' says Erin. 'You know, you're a kind of talisman to the rest of us. I think of you all winter.'

They shouldn't be talking about husbands either.

'Where do they come from,' says Bea, 'the dogs on the beach every day?' Erin doesn't know, any more than anyone knows where the beach-bums come from. Except both are half-wild or half-tame, whichever way you care to see it. Joe brings them a pizza and shrugs politely – he doesn't know either about the dogs. Each day they play, stick-dogs like Merry's drawings, dustbin-robbers, waving tails carried high. They leave messes Worthy investigates with the air of baffled anthropologist: he is a house-dog, these wild scents are not his. Erin says that at the end of the season summer people dump their dogs and a lot die she supposes, but some may breed.

The sun is high and white now. They are dazzled. The island has gone, the lighthouse has gone, they screw up their eyes and just above the line where the horizon would be there is the ghost of a ship shaking in the air. A mirage. A wonder, as if the bright trembling light had lifted the ship on magical fingers.

'Why Marienbad?' yawns Erin.

Bea reflects. 'Not the place. The idea of it. We'd go by train. Take a suite in a wonderful shabby hotel, still quite grand.'

'Delapidated rococo!'

'And spend the morning having massage or our hair combed out. Or drinking disgusting sulphurous waters in a spa where the plants are always nearly dead' (she thinks of Jeannie's conservatory). 'We'd be a mystery, two rich women travelling together.'

'Scandal!' cries Erin, joining in now. 'Could we be lesbians!'

'We eat only white meat and fruit. Young men attend us.'

'Aah.'

Bea thinks perhaps I am getting silly drunk, it's the heat. Maybe I shouldn't play these games with Erin, she looks so wistful. Erin shivers.

'You remember the shanty couple?'

(The girl no one knew with the spiked hair runs always along the beach but she won't be saved she always runs back into the fire. It seems that they must witness this forever. Bea gueses that Erin is thinking of Mercy.)

'There was nothing we could do.' Then: 'Mercy will be fine, you'll see.'

'Yes. Yes, I really think she will, Bea. This summer will do the trick. It's going to be a good season, I feel that.' As usual, when Erin delivers her most optimistic and courageous statements, her brimming eyes contradict her brave smile. 'O, Bea, *children*, what do we do with them?'

Bea thinks of Timbo's face averted, his sweetness, his solemn gentleness with Mercy, the silence from his room, a glance she's caught now and then from some measuring strange who has come to inhabit her son. She doesn't believe in such lumping together but these young, she finds them both enchanting and hard to grasp, with their stillness, soft voices. She regards them with some awe, that they fold their frets quietly away. We made such a fuss. We were so angry. They might have been born at the end of history when gestures become superfluous. The Honda warriors she can at least recognise. Our children speak so quietly one can barely hear what they say.

'Let them go.'

(What about Mercy? She could starve to death. Do you say to Erin: that's her right?)

When two women or three are gathered together they talk about children.

'I thought we weren't talking about children?'

Joe brings them small cups of ferocious black coffee that tastes like treacle. He'll stretch out on the camp bed inside the shack and sleep till five or six.

When Timbo was thirteen or so he slept a lot, he was always tired, and he walked in his sleep. That was terrifying at first. Once he turned up at the Willings's in the middle of the night. Another time Bea found him in the birds' hospital cage on the scorched lawn. Go back to bed said Bea and he went. And he never walked again, to her knowledge. That is the only sign of neurosis he has ever shown.

'I liked having babies,' says Erin. 'I mean having them.'

55

There is a joke here, not sexist, just a fact of nature. Erin is a qualified academic psychologist set fair for a doctorate. Bea in her heyday has stood at Tyre and Egyptian Thebes and Leptis Magna. And these women are talking about babies. They see the joke, they laugh, a little shamefully like men who confess they enjoyed the war.

'Actually,' admits Erin further: 'I found being pregnant rather sexy. The middle months. But people aren't having babies now, had you noticed? That's sad. And us. That part of life's finished.'

For all of us, in a way? thinks Bea: the human race bowing out? Well, there are worse places to do it than on this shore.

That's the rum talking; an alcoholic melancholy which is the disease of this coast, to be fought. But even sober there's a grief about. Is that what's got Herman?

It would be good to have one party like the old days.

Bea may have said this or not. In that extraordinary light and air words were sometimes lost and often that summer the unspoken was understood. Messages were garbled in this ether and others came through with shocking clarity.

Anyway, the women leave the money under a saucer for Joe and go home. That's certain. Something to hold on to. A fact.

Even when they get back the mood of escape is still on them. They unload then flop in the Willings's wild garden drinking the children's blackcurrant juice with ice through straws. Bea lies in the hammock between two pear trees that give nowadays only a sour fruit. 'You're lucky,' she says, 'this green.' 'But we don't have the view.' Buried among the tangle of convolvulus and Queen Anne's lace as tall as trees, there will be the children's plastic toys, mostly Tike and Timbo's guns and tanks. When we're gone, and they excavate this soil, what a warlike race they'll take us for. Francine won't give her children war-toys so they make guns from driftwood: odd how that urge still hangs on though they've grown out of war. Erin puffs and unbuttons to the waist. Bea half-closes her eyes and remembers when they all swam naked at fossil beach and off the lighthouse island, Erin's breasts bobbing happy as seals while Merlyn dived to the sea-bed and at night churning Herman kicked up wonderful phosphorescence. (The telephone rings.) That was another time Francine stripped off, but then we all did: Francine shrieked she was being nibbled by something. Sexy lobster? No. Just Harry Fox underwater. Then Herman, the silver falling off him, caught me round the waist. I think we all made love that night, Harry was noisy, he whooped like a cowboy (the telephone rings): Francine said she nearly drowned.

The telephone rings. Erin and Bea don't answer it, then Erin half-shrugs as though to say, well, that's it, the holiday's over, buttons up and starts for the house and the telephone stops ringing. The Willings's Jeep crunches into the pitted drive, and barely before it has stopped Merry jumps out and flings herself at her mother's skirts: 'My gerbil's broken!' (She must have learned to cry like that from Erin, thinks Bea). 'Oh, sweetheart!' then Erin's crying too. Merlyn lopes towards them, looking tired, carrying in a cardboard box the broken rodent. Poor Jumper may jump no more though the vet's done his best.

'What happened?' says Bea.

'God knows. The vet said a trap or a cat.' With distaste Merlyn hands over the ridiculous leaping mouse and stalks off to Hawkes or Roth or whoever (actually, Erin doesn't know it but Merlyn is a secret novelist. He has been writing a novel for ten years. The third chapter is in its fifteenth draft. The trouble is, he tells himself, that his study of literature has led him to the concept of the perfect novel, a grail he pursues with melancholy fervour. Also, a work so long a'writing is destined to be forever out of date as the rat, time, does his work, Poor Merlyn. Still, as long as he never finishes, who may cast him down?).

Bea, as usual, is left holding the gerbil.

'I kept ringing. There was no reply. When the Willings didn't answer I rang Francine. I even rang Jeannie.'

Bea, just in, flops in the sitting-room rocker. Herman, with his sun-peeled nose, stands over her. She can hardly believe it.

Herman is angry. Then she realises he has been in a panic – he truly feared that because she was a couple of hours late home she had been killed in an accident, plastered all over the coast-road. He's been widowed, forced to make the identification, obliged to arrange the funeral, get a housekeeper, cut short the holiday, deal with the Catarullas and the laundry and the electricity and the milk and the papers. Poor Herman.

'We just went to Joe's.'

'What's that? What have you got in that box?'

'A gerbil.'

A little later he brings her a drink as she's cooking supper. He means sorry. Bea accepts this, and she is sorry too, for thinking the worst of him; she makes up her mind to take back the gerbil in the morning.

Timbo's still out so Herman and Bea eat their meal, wash up together and take their coffee on the porch, side by side. Portrait of a happy couple, watching the sun go down.

4

DAWN.

Merlyn, the secret novelist, is jogging by the sea, trailed by hairless Harry Fox. Jumper the gerbil died in the night, which is probably just as well as it would never have led a full life again. No one blames Bea – after all, she is not a vet. Merry will be consolable with a white kitten from Snowflake Fox's last litter.

Huddled by the breakwaters, the beach-bums stir, draw their rags around them and watch with blank-eyed wonder Merlyn the centaur padding through the spume. Soon they'll be off, they seem to be some species of troglodyte: they spend much of their time in and around the caves above fossil beach. It is not so much the wandering dogs they retreat from (the two packs have much in common) as the summer people in pursuit of sport.

When they first came here the most the summer people had were home-made dinghies and impromptu beach-games. Now there are the dawn joggers, the sand-yachters (at low water), the surfers, the surf-sailors, Francine Fox's purple beach buggy, acrobatic kites and lately hang-gliders from the headland (dangerous game); once Jeannie Fisk took off from the promontory in a hot-air balloon.

There is no colour in the sea or the sky at this first light. It's very still and pure, the joggers a charcoal scrawl. The light plays tricks. You can hear the pug of a mackerel boat but it seems to move very slowly, it will never be gone, it will always be making no progress through the milky water towards the lighthouse and the ocean.

Toby floats on his back, grateful for the salty support: out of his depth, he is not a particularly good swimmer. He looks down his flat stomach, empty, and relishes a kind of ascetic virtue in his breakfastlessness. He's no anexoriac but reflects sometimes that it would be invigorating to do without everything (well, almost everything). To walk shoeless, to go as near as possible foodless and roofless. Wryly, he realises that he is not yet free to put on such monkish ways: he must live for a while yet – at least three-quarters live – in his parents' furnished world. He doesn't mind that too much. But he rarely uses pot, has never smoked, drinks nothing more than beer and has secret plans to pare down the trappings of his life. (He's no Puritan, no proselytiser, only wishes his mother would give up smoking so that she might not die of cancer). He won't join the beach-bums or any commune because that seems to him just huddling together in the dark, no better than the games the old people play.

Toby realises this may be the last summer with his parents. At the same moment he has thought to himself: well, I might do that, or live like this, he has grasped their vulnerability. It's not easy. Perhaps he will take this summer to think, to look around.

A clump of Japanese seaweed sails past tangled with shit.

Toby adjusts himself with a kick to keep himself floating and looks between his toes. There is the beach awakening: shutters are flung open and Francine comes out on the balcony with the little Foxes. There's Merlyn jogging with Harry. A figure he can't make out, Mercy or Erin, is down on the hard below the Willings's house. Jeannie's villa on the promontory is too far to judge if the blinds are up. They are, he guesses; he knows Jeannie doesn't sleep so well – she told him, as women, his mother's friends, do tell him things. He used to be a little bored or embarrassed by this, then he was flattered, now Toby simply accepts it. It dawns on Toby that he likes women, he finds them interesting. It may be that his childhood was spent mostly in the company of his mother – his father was and is permanently airborne.

For the first six years of his life Toby believed his father to be an airline pilot. Then Herman tried to explain the workings of a multinational company but Toby, normally a receptive child, went deaf with disappointment. For a while he even kept going a fantasy that his father was dead: so convinced was he of the reality of this invention, Toby at some point between the ages of six and ten actually planned a future for Bea and himself. They would leave the city and live permanently at the beach-house. He would fish and when he got old enough he would work fitting out boats. He and Bea would start an animal and bird hospital run on Robin Hood principles – the rich paying, the poor and the wild treated free. When Herman turned up from one of his circum-navigations of the earth this set back Toby's plans. He didn't mope for long because that summer Herman taught him to sail.

Toby has talked to Mercy about this.

'You know, I felt I'd betrayed her. That's crazy. I suppose it's because I'm the only one.'

'Everyone's the only one. It's normal.'

There have been times lately when Toby has felt this place to be unreal. He looks between his toes and would not be surprised to see the whole scene dissolve. The heat is rising. The earth begins to shake, the air trembles, he's hungry after all and a little chilled.

The family Tyler have breakfast. That is, that must be, real. Bea drops two yellow eggs in the pan. The percolator is blue. There is a scent of coffee. The earthenware is peasant-pastoral: patterned with coloured fruits, glazed, a little lumpy. There is also the texture of the pine kitchen table, grained and knotted but smooth to the touch. There is a green glass jug of orange juice and a white, blue-banded jug of milk that speaks to Bea of childhood and deep grass and celandines and shaded dairies (the milk comes in litres from the hyper-market, it is the jug that sanctifies).

'I remember a jug like that,' she says and Timbo looks interested (politeness?) but she cannot explain, she cannot recall where she saw a jug like that before, if she ever did. She bought this one in the city at one of those ferociously expensive little shops that cater for the nostalgia of people like her. (Amazing how such places flourish – you can't be sure of the water supply or bread or electricity or gas or doctors or ambulances or fire-fighters or police or public transport, but at a price French provincial gratin dishes, fish kettles and Victorian commodes are always available. Jeannie says there's a warehouse somewhere for the middle-class bourgeoisie. Maybe she's right. Dispossessed spiritually, thinks Bea, we seek lares and penates, search for the numinous in the furnishings of the dead. Somewhere or other the desperate houseless have taken over a necropolis, a city of the dead supplied with everything but cooking and sewage facilities, for obvious reasons.)

Earlier, she gave the dreadful cat a raw egg and, having napped on the porch, he'll be out now killing. He's a gangster.

Herman and Timbo eat their eggs. Bea crumbles a croissant, wonders about baking bread.

'It's good weather for the party.'

'Party?' says Herman. He does not want to go to a party.

'Only the Willings. You don't mind the Willings.'

'No,' he says, 'if Erin lays off the garlic. It's just that I don't feel like a party.'

Toby looks at his mother. He looks at his father. In a mug at the centre of the table there are wild daisies, one of the few flowers, along with poppies, that grow on the dry hinterland: indoors they give off an acrid scent. From his early-morning swim Toby carries within him the idea of disintegration. He closes his eyes, opens them and sees the green glass jug shatter, the table tip, Herman clutch his chest and crash to the floor, Bea's hand pour blood, the floor awash with orange and milk, the windows fly out. The pretty peasant plates whirl around the room. Ho, cackles the wicked witch of the north and they are all turned to stone.

'Erin says those dogs are wild.'

'But if you want to go.'

'People just dump them at the end of the season. I think that's terrible, don't you? You don't have to come.' With her second cup of coffee Bea lights her first cigarette.

'What dogs?'

'The dogs on the beach.'

'I don't know why we have these parties.'

Bea begins to stack the plates. She pauses and looks at her husband. This place has never failed before to work for any of them. She has this idea of magic, a magical place. Fantastical. She likes that word. She is an optimist. There is something dry in her and something hopeful.

She measures her words. 'We don't have to have any parties at all,' she says reasonably. 'But Timbo and I promised to help Erin.'

She wishes she could help Herman. But apparently not. They have this famous marriage, but it doesn't seem much use at the moment. The tachycardia hasn't bothered him lately, she knows that because he hasn't been taking the tablets, yet Herman this morning reminds her of Worthy Willings on a hot day – though Worthy, in dog years, is seventy to Herman's fifty.

Bea wonders if her husband could be turning into one of her lame dogs.

She touches his hand. 'Why don't you take the lugger out for the day?'

Bea and Timbo wash up. Herman takes the paper on to the porch, but he doesn't read it. He looks at the ocean and sees a super-jumbo hurtling slowly across the sky. How many thousand miles does he fly a year? The air, more than the earth, has become his element, yet each time on take-off he still feels like Icarus, flying too high and sure to fall. He thinks of a neutron war breaking out while he's airborne, of earthquakes, of tidal waves, of his home planet becoming hostile territory. It wouldn't surprise him to hear that the Company has made provision for this. It has made provision for everything else, including revolution, a pension scheme tagged to the cost of living, a counter-industrial-espionage squad equipped with bugging devices to bug the opposition's bugs, a payola fund for left, right, middle, Mafia, black power, white militants, Chinese communists and Greek police, and the sudden onset of flying phobia among middle-aged executives.

Herman rubs his peeling nose. He squints at the sky. The paper says SAUDI ARABIA GOES WET A FAIR DEAL FOR PAEDOPHILIACS WEST COAST QUAKE KILLS SIXTY.

One absurd, unasked-for and unintelligible phrase keeps running through Herman's mind as he regards the ocean: we have our backs to the sea.

'Apporhais,' Bea tells Mercy. 'Jurassic gastropod'.

'It's beautiful.'

The woman and the girl sit bare-footed below the porch, Bea's fossil-drawer between them. With her long, thin, breakable fingers Mercy touches divine Aporrhais. Rare. North Atlantic. But Bea Tyler found it on fossil beach, chipped away and there she lay in her dark bed, queen of them all.

Mercy has always been fascinated by Bea's fossils ever since she was a child and long before she could have understood their significance. Though Bea has pointed out and named them and Mercy knows their names, their provenance, the pleasure she has in them seems to be tactile rather than palaeontological. She loves to touch them and to hold them. Mercy is good with the broken birds too, though at the moment the hospital cage is empty. Mercy herself could do with mending, it strikes Bea, but she cannot think however to go about it.

After a while Mercy says: 'I love it here.'

'Yes, we're all very lucky.'

'No. I mean here. In your house.'

Bea lets the sand run through her fingers, smiles and thinks of all the things she might say, remembers Mercy as a child, when she would suddenly stop playing and come and sit quietly by her side, like this. And on hot nights Mercy and Timbo slept out on the porch. Mercy used to talk to Bea then. She hasn't talked to her for a long time, not since she stopped eating. Whose fault is this? Mercy's or Bea's?

Mercy goes on: 'It's so peaceful.'

Deploring the beach-dogs, Worthy Willings comes and flops between them; he looks at the woman and the girl, grunts with satisfaction: he's too old for children, cats, and defending his territorial imperative.

Mercy means, no one fights here. Bea might have answered, it's not half as peaceful as you think, there's something dangerous around this summer. But they are constrained by loyalties, principally to Erin. Bea cannot ask and Mercy cannot answer that life in the ménage Willings is more or less intolerable, like living as a civilian in a war-zone. It goes without saying, though.

Bea leans back against the porch and through half-closed eyes sees Mercy smooth the little patch of sand; then she collects a handful of pebbles and presses them carefully on to the surface of the sand in a square; a pebble roof is added, a chimney, pebble windows and door. Mercy has made a house. Now she makes a wall of pebbles and within it sets a garden of shells. Still not satisfied, she plucks a few heads of sea lavender and plants them in the garden. With her finger she traces a curl of smoke from the chimney. Mercy has made a home.

She rubs it out before any one can see.

Mercy hugs Worthy. 'Virginia Woolf says Thomas Hardy had a dog called Wessex.'

'What a mouthful. No worse than Worthy though, I suppose.' At the mention of his name, Worthy grins. Even in the shade he's panting. Bea fetches him a dish of water, the cat's dish.

Mercy will not be helping get the food together for tonight, obviously, though she may hang some paper lanterns in the trees.

'It's not that I don't want to eat,' she tells Bea, 'It's that I *can't.*'

Erin would pack Mercy off to the past-life therapy man. Jeannie would snort. Timbo tempts her with apples. Bea wonders if any of them have any right to tell Mercy: you must live. Or is that just another sentimental fallacy?

Bea imagines shaking Mercy by those bird-bone shoulders and telling her: you have this precious gift of life!

(Which may suddenly be withdrawn – as Jumper would testify, if the dead could speak. If gerbils could speak.)

The sky and the sea and the land are divided into bold blocks of colour from a child's paint-box, just as though everything were simple.

'Come on,' says Bea. 'They're beaching the lugger.'

Tears are streaming down Erin's flushed face but it's only onions.

She's standing over the turkey with a hammer.

'Oh God,' she says, 'I forgot to defrost it, Bea.'

Erin weeps in the middle of her party food, all in various stages of preparation. She's run out of pots and the spaghetti's in a bucket. The kitchen is an oily furnace in which garlic reigns overall. Merlyn stalks through carrying a crate of wine. If he weren't so handsome he would look like a bistro waiter in denims, matelot top and red neck-scarf. He may be looking for an axe to kill his wife. He may be writing the definitive novel of this half-century or remembering Francine Fox's silky thighs, if there is any truth in that story Jeannie Fisk puts about. He is actually thinking that he would rather go to a party in a novel than give one. Updike people give good parties. He could take Francine? Bea takes the turkey and the hammer from Erin, she puts the hammer in a drawer and sets the turkey to soak in its plastic bag in cold water. It says on the bag: TO DEFROST SOAK IN BAG IN COLD WATER.

'*Cold* water!' cries Erin. 'O, Bea, I never thought of that.'

Bea and Erin work in the kitchen. Timbo's out in the garden with Mercy, setting up tables and hanging paper lanterns. Bea brings some order to the kitchen and after a while the two women work peaceably, almost enjoying the frying and the boiling and the roasting. So many dead animals, thinks Bea, and remembers a story she and Timbo used to read when he was small: "And Mrs Pig went to market and said: a pound of person please."

That became a family joke.

They could hardly keep straight faces in the butcher's.

Now they are more or less vegetarian, though they're not silly about it. Herman, who never really took in the joke in the first place, likes meat or rather he thinks blood might keep at bay the bad fairy Anaemia. However he prefers lean cuts and avoids cholesterol, of course.

About five, Bea and Erin collapse, gulping iced cooking sherry. (Bea thinks: we all seem to be drinking a lot this summer. There is something sad about women drinking in kitchens.)

They take their glasses into the deep green garden. Erin fans her face with a leaf and says: 'I'm so terribly sorry about Francine.'

'?' For a moment Bea thinks that Erin means the rumoured business between Merlyn and Francine. Surely Jeannie hasn't been such a bitch.

'Well, she *is* an alcoholic, isn't she?'

'She does drink a bit too much. Maybe we all do?'

'She's so lovely. Francine's so lovely.'

So either there is no truth in the story, or Erin doesn't know the story, or Erin is a saint or an idiot.

Either way, Bea wants to get off the subject of Francine.

'Erin, if I'm going to bath and change I'd better go.'

'Oh Bea, thank you, bless you! I know now everything will be fine?'

'It'll be fine.' Bea slips her unfinished drink under a clump of laurel. She sees Timbo waiting for her and is astonished as always by his height. They're all like that now: long-boned – something in the food? A genetic re-adjustment? They're like something from SF or Grimm, these giant children.

Erin is calling something after her.

'I said, why do we give these parties?'

'Because we always have.'

Bea and Timbo walk home along the beach. They walk through the soapy fringe of tide. Bea carries her espadrilles, Timbo has his, the laces tied together, strung round his neck. When the mother speaks, the son dips to hear her like a young stork.

Bea says: 'When we first came here we slept in a tent, you wouldn't remember. There was nothing but the shack and Jeannie's house – though Jeannie wasn't there, of course. Oh, and the Willings's house, before the Willings. I forget who lived there.'

Toby wonders why they always talk about the past. He finds that rather sad. They're not so old: his mother isn't old at all (he prefers not to think of her being old; he no longer expects his parents to be cut down by violence, eaten by bears, immolated – though that accident on the coast-road shook him. Toby does though, he realises, fear their deaths. Precisely, he fears his mother's death-bed. It's a terrible thing, but he wishes for both their sakes she might be carried away suddenly and painlessly, he's not sure he has the stamina for her dying. In a way he feels, either he must leave entirely, soon, orphaning himself, or put himself into training now for her death. Sometimes there seems no third option).

Sometimes he wishes they would die now and get it over with.

Bea remembers when they first saw this coast and put up their tent and camped out, on and off, a whole summer, while the beach-house went up. Herman came down at weekends. They knew no one – there was no one to know, except the couple in the fishing-shack. With their backs to the land, sitting on the beach looking at the ocean, Bea and Herman were happy and awed: as if they had come upon some prelapsarian heaven.

On weekdays, when she was alone with Timbo, a baby, Bea found that she adjusted to a different clock, rising and going to bed early, exploring the rock pools in the morning, swimming while Timbo slept, in the afternoon reading and dozing in the wonderful green light of the tent. She got to know the fishing-shack couple, thought not well. Sometimes they brought her a fish. Sometimes the girl would smile, then after a while she would baby-sit while Bea explored fossil beach. They never talked much. Bea thought the girl might have been pretty, but she had cold sores at the corner of her mouth and broken finger-nails. Bea had the impression that the boy might be dodging some draft, they both had the air of fugitives and when Herman was there they never came over at all. They were like a pair of shy and tattered birds driven here by some desperate storm. It was hard to see how they lived, but they did live. The girl even put up cheap curtains. On a still night Bea from her tent could hear them mewing with love, like sea-gulls, though not, alas, half as tough. Then suddenly they burned to death, but that was later.

There was a burst of excavation around here a few years ago: for oil and other secrets. They found no oil but turned up some shale beads, the poor man's jet, together with a little drinking-cup. Then the diggers and the drillers went away and the earth healed.

Toby feels remorse that he should have half-wished her death upon his mother. He weighs her up and decides she is in pretty good condition anyway, so there is probably nothing to worry about.

Besides, they have a good relationship. They get on well, he realises that, better than most. He doesn't think about it much, but sometimes he looks around at his friends and their mothers and is shocked by the way they go on – you'd think they hated each other and maybe they do. It's embarrassing. He has perfectly reasonable friends who behave like madmen with their mothers. Tike, for instance (that is, Timothy Willings) – he's seen Tike make Erin cry (admittedly everything makes Erin cry, not a sparrow falls but her eyes brim); and Erin seemed to be goading Tike to make her cry. That was really terrible, Toby felt worse about it in a way than Tike or Erin. It was an absurd little scene about nothing but Toby felt as if a door had been opened upon chaos. He felt like an observer at a war. He didn't know it but he was feeling the shame and the guilt of the witness – fear too, that there might be something in himself that licked bloody fangs: an unwilled response to violence.

Now Timbo and Bea are nearly home. They will change and go to the party, with or without Herman, whether or not they wish to, for Erin's sake, and Mercy's too.

One of the beach-dogs is barking at their heels, playing grandmother's footsteps, retreating and yapping when they turn round. The animal looks starved, but it's no use: how could you feed them all, ever? And it might well bite your hand off. Some wild things are unadoptable.

Toby stands, kicking the shingle, for some reason reluctant to follow Bea into the house, and wash, and feed the cat, and so on. Suddenly he realises that maybe his friends make war for the small issues because they anticipate escalation.

He is afraid that one day Bea might make some claim on him, cry; I gave you life so give me yours! Hardly. Bea is not that kind of person.

Toby shrugs and goes indoors to change. Why not? Next year he'll probably be somewhere else.

There is just one moment, round now when the dogs have gone and before the sleepers arrive, that the beach is empty, as it was when the Tylers found it, before the couples and the houses and the parties and the dogs came, before Joe and Jeannie and the bums and the fire. When no one possessed it, before it was spoiled.

There is the party.

Merlyn the secret novelist, while deploring this party, thinks that a party might make a very good structure for a novel: it would observe the unities, have a beginning, a middle and an end. In the depths of his secret heart, where sentiment and innocence lurk, Merlyn is, in literary matters, a closet traditionalist.

Does he believe then in heroes and heroines? If so, which would qualify of those wending their way to the Willings' party through the bright early evening?

None of them, probably, though each might have his moment: this is life.

Some come from the coast road, some from the beach on foot. There is a distinction between the two (except for Jeannie Fisk who defies every distinction because she is Jeannie). The first-comers, for instance, are always the Bonifaces who don't exactly count because they are not beach-people. On the other hand, he is a paediatrician with the face of Saint Sebastian pierced by arrows (his clients' small fierce problems?). She is appalling but for the sake of Tonio Boniface one tries to be nice to them. (Besides, one never knows when Tonio might come in – so handy to have an expert up the hill.)

Merlyn opens bottles of red plonk. Erin, wearing a butcher's apron and a high colour straight from the kitchen, carrying a knife, embraces Betty Boniface; Betty was a student of Merlyn's once, met Tonio here, gobbled him up whole and has since been permanently pregnant. As soon as she sees Merlyn she sits at his feet. He is hiding from her in his study. The Foxes arrive, Erin flings the Bonifaces at the Foxes, leaves them in the garden looking at vegetables and rings Bea from the telephone in the downstairs loo. Bea must come soon, at once, she cries! 'The Bonifaces are boring the Foxes in the garden and you know Betty. I was carrying a knife!' 'Erin, you haven't knifed Betty Boniface?' 'I've got to go now, Bea. Poor Tonio – he is rather sweet.' 'He didn't *have* to marry Betty.' 'Bea? Bea, are you there? *Bea, I can't give this party!*' 'I'll be over soon, Erin. We're all coming.'

Bea sighs and hangs up. Herman raises his eyebrows. Bea explains: 'Erin may have knifed Betty Boniface, but I doubt it.'

Herman nods. He's a gentle man. He is touched by Erin, provided he doesn't actually have to deal with her. Well, he has his own problems, hasn't he? Getting ready for the party, he sticks out his tongue in front of the kitchen mirror. Is it a little furry? Herman takes literally the confession: there is no health in us.

He used to enjoy these parties. Either he has changed or the parties have changed. Herman remembers the time they all went out to the lighthouse island and swam in the phosphorescence, shaking the silver like scales from their bodies, and he kissed Erin or it might have been Francine, and love was made. He made love to Bea, his feet on the bottom, her legs round his waist. They were all glorious then. Bea says she would like to give another party like that, this year. Herman rubs his chin, decides not to shave, and thinks: if we went back would we find our former selves, and could we bear it?

'Should I shave?' Herman asks Bea. 'No', she says, touches his cheek with her finger. 'You're lucky, your colouring.' But the few bristles there are she has noticed lately are grey, while his hair is still sand (a man made of sand, she thinks, like a golden snowman, could melt — she sees Herman for a flash as he sees himself: this man who seems so solid dissolving, sand running through your fingers, sandman). Timbo has started shaving a couple of times a week — like Herman he will always have a light beard. Herman used to talk about growing a beard and it would have suited him, but the Company would have disapproved. The Company disapproves of any flamboyant self-image. Now it's too late. If Herman grew a beard it would be grey.

Coming into the kitchen Toby is aware of a complicity between his parents. He wonders how he feels about this. Surely he's glad, because then he can leave them without a scruple? He's slightly thrown to recognise that there might be something bleak and alarming even about this freedom.

Toby remembers hearing his parents talking to one couple who couldn't abide their children and couldn't wait for them to get out of the house. And another couple liked theirs but lived for the day when they'd fly the nest. Even now, among adults, it still happened: they forgot that Toby was there with his two ears cocked.

Toby stands in the pretty kitchen in the evening sun and imagines his parents arm-in-arm on the porch crying Go! And then, Come back! Which does he want to hear?

The world does not stand still, of course, for Toby Tyler. While he dithers at the crossroads Herman could be felled by death (for some reason, Toby always imagines his father going out abruptly, dying, as they say, suddenly in the night); leaving Toby with the responsibility for Bea. Bea as poor old grey-haired mother rocking to death on the porch? Hardly.

Just as Toby is about to follow his parents out of the house the telephone rings and it's some wild woman keening. Just as she is cut off he recognises her as the female of the Catarullas who took their house for the summer. Toby looks at the telephone. He imagines the house in the city, the mid-summer garbage in the gutters, the drab, dusty trees, the foreigners, the sirens in the night. That woman sounds mad. She might burn down the house.

The Tyler family walk along the beach to the party. The cat follows them. It has not killed today. How lucky they are to be walking by the ocean! Bea looks back, smiles, takes Timbo's arm.

'Solemn?'

'Nothing.'

'This summer's not much fun for you, is it? Maybe you should have gone to camp with Tike. Or if Tike had been here.'

'It's fine.' Toby knows exactly how it would have been if Tike Willings had been here. All Tike is interested in nowadays is losing his virginity. So is Toby, up to a point, but last summer was a bore, chasing girls on Tike's Yamaha. The yacht club girls were pretty but dull, they had long brown legs and pin-heads; the town girls could be met only at the disco: they looked old in purple with white lips and destroyed hair, but half of them were twelve and while Tike said they were hot Toby felt like a baby-sitter. Which left the troglodyte beach-sleepers, a few of whom did strike Toby as interesting beneath the dust of centuries (literally – those caves on fossil beach are Jurassic at least, possibly Permian). But there weren't so many of them last summer and they were either attached, or they had this habit if you spoke to them of smiling but never answering, as if words might damage the air, or their lips had

73

been magically sealed. Toby does still wonder about them, though; he's never wanted to join them and doubts if he'd lose his virginity there (there is something asexual about them), but a couple of times he has taken down a few oranges, as an offering, and sat by them in silence. It was restful but not, he felt, a way of life.

Even Tike grew dispirited after a while. Indignant, in fact —what an affliction to be a seventeen-year-old virgin in this day and age! It was unnatural! A desperate affair!

'Well, we're the two wise virgins,' said Toby.

Tike kicked sand in his face and raced into the sea.

'If it goes on like this it'll be rape,' said Tike.

Toby wonders if Tike's getting on any better at camp. If Tike has disposed of his virginity, Toby wonders if he will mind being the one wise virgin.

Bea, still thinking that Timbo should have the company of young people, says: 'There's always the Boniface boys, I suppose.'

Toby pulls a face and so does Bea. The two eldest Bonifaces, Wayne and Darren, a little younger than Timbo, were brought up when permissiveness was still the rage (Tonio was one of the gurus of children's lib, wrote *Kids Rule OK* and was responsible for a quite monstrous regiment of liberated toddlers. He's into authority now but too late for Wayne and Darren who can still strip a house bare in half an hour. They used to pull the wings off Toby's model aircraft and the legs off his soldiers).

There is a rumour that Wayne Boniface is an accident of Merlyn's, when Betty was his student. Certainly Betty and Tonio married in haste and Wayne was a seven-month baby.

The party begins. The Tylers take a deep breath and push open the Willings's lattice gate. Too late now to turn back. Betty Boniface, wearing pink stretch slacks, is not lying in the vegetable plot with a knife in her back but boring Harry Fox about the death of the novel. Francine, looking glorious in what appears to be a number of loosely connected chiffon scarves, signals frantically from behind Betty's back. 'Bea, Herman, thank God you're here.' On the pretext of embracing, she gets them to the kitchen door and hisses: 'Erin's locked herself in the loo and Merlyn won't come out!' 'Merlyn's in the loo with Erin?' Momentarily, the Tylers are confused but they sort it out. More people are arriving. Herman is sent to take drinks out to them, Toby goes to look for Mercy; Harry Fox, escaped from Betty, volunteers to carve while Francine lays out plates (she'll break a few, she's high on something but not drunk, Bea judges). Keep them outside, Bea tells Herman and goes to talk to Erin. 'Erin,' says Bea to the loo door, 'Erin, are you there? You must come out.' A wail and a snuffle. Bea remembers there is a small medicine cabinet in the downstairs lavatory. 'Erin – you haven't taken anything?' Another snuffle then silence. 'Erin, have you swallowed something? Please tell me.' Bea settles on the floor and wishes she had brought a drink and an ashtray. There's an ashtray in the loo. For a mad moment she thinks of asking Erin to open the door and pass her the ashtray. It occurs to her that someone else may wish to use the lavatory, may observe that she is sitting on the floor talking to the door. 'Erin?' 'Oh, Bea, I can't give this party!' 'You've no choice, Erin. The party's started.' Herman tiptoes up behind Bea together with both Foxes, all performing a pantomime of silence. Harry whispers: 'Toby found Mercy who got Merlyn to come out.' Bea nods and puts her finger to her lips. They all listen to the door. Suddenly Erin giggles. 'You'd never believe it! I've found my old diaphragm – it's in shreds! Lord, Bea, do you remember diaphragms? We put them in for parties. I mean years ago. We washed them in pure soap and dusted them with powder.' The tears are spurting again as Erin cries so faintly they have to crane to hear: 'Oh, Bea, what happened?' Bea sighs, lets Harry Fox light her cigarette, closes her eyes for a blink, sees all their lives falling away. Merlyn appears, takes them all in and clearly finds them absurd, stalks up to the door and raps twice: 'Erin, will you open this door.' The lavatory flushes, Erin opens the door and comes out, smiling tremulously. They all go back to the party. Bea finds she is shaking, but she has a drink and then she's fine.

Bea was right. A party has its own momentum. There is a point, about an hour into a party, when it takes on a life of its own, independent of its begetters who are powerless now to halt it. There was a moment when Erin might have been found dead in the loo, but she wasn't, nor did Betty bleed to death among the cabbages, nothing happened.

So Erin patches up her face and moves among her guests wearing her Charley Brown smile and a Be Happy button. She enjoys parties and now the party is running under its own steam all she has to do is to check from time to time that everyone has enough to eat and drink. Everyone is startled by the quantity of food (well, the women are), and just for once Erin's wistful vision of bountifulness seems nearly realised (her own daughter, indeed, appears to be the one person who will not feast at her table). This is spring, dusk comes around eight or so, the guests sup the soft twilight, wade in the wild garden through drifts of blossom. They should be speaking of philosophy or God but it's mostly gossip. There is a bark of laughter. Someone is playing a recorder rather well, a thin air. Mercy and Timbo move among the trees lighting the fairy lamps. Betty Boniface has finally cornered Merlyn and demands to know about the death of the novel. She is pregnant again and the pink stretch bulge comes between her and Merlyn and the possibility of a meaningful tutorial. Merlyn – who has a vested interest in the survival of the novel of which Betty wots not – is mellowed by wine and decides to give her exactly what she asks for, though not what she wants. 'The novel,' he says, 'lives,' and he wonders how he could ever have capered among the filing cabinets with this perfectly awful woman. As a girl she was athletic, he remembers sorely –she sprained his toe. 'What are you talking about?' There, thank God, is Francine, a little lop-sided in the quince. Come with me, my sexy silky love and we'll live in a novel! 'Death. We were talking about death.' 'Who's dead?' 'Betty says the novel is dead.' 'Oh, you were having a *literary* conversation.' Francine pulls a face. 'Don't let me stop you. Go on. I'll listen.' (It is well known that Francine cannot read.) Francine never uses her sex consciously, she is too guileless for that; nor does she dislike Betty though Betty dislikes her because she considers her ill-read and unstable. Betty is routed. Merlyn allows Francine to bite his neck.

Bea sees Francine Fox biting Merlyn and steers Harry Fox away to another part of the garden. Harry has short square hands and he is the best porch-builder on the beach. Bea asks him about computers. Harry says there are already computers that can talk only to each other. No one can understand them but they contain such vital information they cannot be scrapped. The worst thing is, they are decision-making computers. Harry looks so worried, and no wonder, for these computers are part of the defence and retaliation system of this hemisphere. Their decisions cannot be countermanded because it would take another computer to work out the implications of countermanding their decisions 'and we won't get that much time, Bea.' 'No, I suppose not.' Bea finds it hard to believe that this stolid, practical, anxious man is such a monster in bed, but who knows how anyone is in bed? That is one of life's great mysteries. Harry says the computers, who are called Snoopy and Woodstock, have written a novel. 'What was it like?' 'Lousy.'

Mercy sits on the old swing under the apple tree, her tangled hair crossed in two sad wings beneath her chin: a girl of elaborate sorrows, you might guess, though they all look like that nowadays. There is a glass of lemon beside her, undrunk. Toby sprawls at her feet dreaming of some clean new place, a virgin beach of untrod sand. His mother says this place was like that once and it probably was.

There is a hiatus. There always is about now.

'Food! Food!' cries Erin, suddenly anxious that her guests should eat everything, she can't bear anything to be left, not one scrap (perhaps she has seen Francine nibbling Merlyn and fears an outbreak of cannibalism). 'Food!' cries Erin and her pins drop and her hair falls down and her trailing sleeves are snatched by twigs and trees and shrubs and raspberry canes as she beats her wild garden in search of the starving to feed.

Mercy shudders. No wonder she can't eat. From where they sit, a little above the rest of the garden, Toby observes the luxuriance. From this vantage the vegetation could be more important than the people – certainly it's more vigorous than these carnivorous bipeds. In the twilight everything green and growing assumes a greater stature and authority: the people are dwarfed, nature rules as she must once have done on the whole face of the earth. Bea has said: it's never really been man's – the earth. We're here on sufferance. Any day we could be frozen out or broiled alive. Toby didn't think much about what she said at the time, but walking city pavements at the age of thirteen he was suddenly and quite alarmingly aware of the eras beneath his feet, which might abruptly claim their kingdoms: Palaeozoic, Mesozoic, Caenozoic – the three wicked sisters who could at any moment topple that skyscraper, crack and devour everything concrete and plastic and wood and stone, all the works of man (Bea omitted to mention that she was talking in millions or billions of years, the takeover would not be tomorrow).

Something is in the wind. Canines are not what they used to be, the Tylers' dentist says. Meat may be on the way out.

Here, in this garden between the hinterland and the ocean, you might imagine that you have come upon a last tribe – that's how it strikes Toby, just for a minute. This could be how it would end. That's a fancy that used to frighten him, but now he finds it rather fascinating. (Ho ho, you are doomed, all doomed, the sea is poisoned, the earth is dead!) It is not annihilation that intrigues him – he quite enjoys being alive – so much as the behaviour of mankind upon its last beach.

Worthy Willings joins Mercy and Toby. He's too old a dog for parties. When they have drink taken, people either stand on him or pat him too hard or feed him unsuitable food.

At last Jeannie Fisk has arrived – not on a broomstick but

from the ocean. Her motor boat is anchored off-shore and she rows in, stepping ashore in her thrown-on priceless pants suit which is damp at the hem. She knows the Willings's plonk and has brought her own vodka. 'Take my painter, Fox,' she says, and strides up the beach.

With Jeannie's arrival, the party moves into its third stage, thickens, coagulates: indoors, outdoors, on the beach, there are intense knots of talk. Bea moves between them, wondering what she is seeking and what escapes her. A certainty? A form, a purpose? The dusk puts identities in doubt. She feels among strangers, a visitant, yearns for something clear and sure, but the light here always defeats her. It is always too light or too dark.

'Well, yes, the therapy of violence,' Tonio Boniface is saying, standing under a tree on one leg, doing an elaborate conjuring trick with glass, plate and thin black cigar. He has a long, enquiring nose and the yellow complexion of an El Greco.

'Like the S.P.K.? The patients' collective? I remember!' Erin is fired. Frantic for Mercy, she who should know better runs from the idea of one therapy to another: at this moment she is quite capable of handing Mercy a gun. If she had a gun. If Tonio hadn't wagged his head. The toddlers' liberator is for law and order now. Besides, Germany is a special case.

'Wasn't that the Baader-Meinhof lot?'

'They liberated hospital patients.'

'They let the loonies loose.'

'And look what happened.'

'What did happen?'

'Germany has always been a special case.'

'Yum – this sauce.'

'Where did you get this ham?'

'Have you *seen* Jeannie Fisk?'

'I like Germany.'

' – walked to the window, opened it, and just jumped out!'

'That's the most *fantastic* material.'

' – I tell you, there she was talking about vegetables; hold my glass she says and out she goes: splat.'

'Lovely garden. Erin's lucky. All we grow is thorns. Poor Erin.'

'Splat!'

Jeannie Fisk is terrible, marvellous too. She might have been a character they invented, when the time was ripe, who got out of hand. They wanted a catalyst and got a monster.

Only Bea does not see Jeannie as a monster because she does not believe in monsters; any more than she believes that Mercy is bound to go splat.

'But what about Hitler?' Well, yes, there was Hitler. Tonio Boniface can go on as much as he likes about the expression of a national psychosis yet the fact remains, Hitler was. He peed and roared and slept like anyone and went to parties.

Francine Fox knows someone who knows someone who saw Hitler in a South American café, although even if he had survived the bunker he would by now be a long time dead.

Do you believe in ghosts?

Bea is feeling a little odd tonight. Nothing would surprise her, even Hitler. Who's to say we're real, she thinks? We could all be phantasms. The idea is entertaining, for if we are dead we cannot die.

It's the light, she decides, and goes indoors, finds Jeannie sitting on the loo, with the door unlocked. She's reading one of the paperbacks from the shelf behind the cistern and sipping vodka from a tooth-mug. Come in, come in, she says, help yourself, God, I hate novels.

'Do you believe in ghosts?' says Bea. Yes, vodka is much better.

'I believe in sex, death and money.'

Bea sits on the floor, her legs stretched out straight in front of her, smoking and sipping vodka. As far as she is concerned, most of this party so far seems to be taking place in the lavatory.

'The thing is, if you were a ghost would you know you were?'

'Look,' says Jeannie. 'We're born. We die. We don't get back. That's all.'

Someone is rapping on the door. Knock knock who's there? It sounds urgent.

Jeannie stands, hitches up her pants, drops the paperback down the lavatory pan, flushes. So much for the novel.

'Who was it?' says Bea.

'Hemingway.'

Poor Ernest.

It's Betty Boniface outside. Pregnancy makes her pee.

Tonio Boniface is really very sweet. He holds court among mothers though he must have quite enough in the week of bed-wetting, thumb-sucking, dyslexia, undescended testicles, sibling rivalry, allergy, nappy rash, birth trauma and infantile somnambulism. He is under the same tree but sitting down now, cross-legged (his knees nearly touch his ears), with the mothers squatting around him in a circle. They look, Bea thinks, like children at a picnic. When Tonio came out for potty training and against demand feeding it was almost like the heady days of Spock's recantation, for anyone who could remember that. Jeannie rolls her eyes: that fake! Bea smiles, thinks how beautiful it is here at this time of night this season of the year, hears the party humming well, slips through the wicket gate where the party has already begun to spill out onto the sand, and remembers the seasons of this beach; the year Jeannie (before she renounced the novel) saw herself as mistress of a salon and filled the beach with intellectuals – they had sharp knees and peeling noses, played violent ball games, and everyone that summer was writing a book or reviewing a book or getting over writing a book or breaking down after writing a book. The ocean came in and out, the sun shone, the light stung and Merlyn Willings sulked, to be only a grain of sand among so many. Then Jeannie chucked them out, or they just went. One morning they were gone, taking their words with them in duffle bags and rucksacks and matched luggage and carrier bags, and inside the little bone temples of their heads.

Bea kicks off her sandals. Voices from the garden are very clear. She paddles in the cool sand, white as snow by moonlight. Though the Willings's house is angled the wrong way for a view of the ocean, its situation at the corner of the beach below the cliff shelters it to some degree from winter storms and the sun's killing eye, so here there are greenness and glints of gold, birds and flowers, goldcrest, greenfinch, celandine by the thin fresh-water stream that runs from the cliff and irrigates the garden before it is turned to salt.

There is a squeal from the garden: Betty Boniface has found Hemingway in the loo. Toby is being polite to Jeannie Fisk – he's a polite boy. Yes, he says, he'll be going to college, but not next year. Next year he'll just look around. Actually, she's not so bad really, people hardly ever are when you come to know them. At least the Fisk woman seems to know who she is, which is more than you can say for most of them on the beach. Perhaps he should go to America? There was a time when everyone seemed to be going to America and somehow Toby had assumed that when the moment came he too would go. Then no one, if they could avoid it, seemed to go to America any more, or India, or anywhere: it was as though they had decided to stay at home and pull the curtains and bolt the door and put up the storm shutters and bring in the cat.

Mercy did not so much walk away as dissolve, when Jeannie Fisk collared Toby. He feels a little guilty about that. Mercy in the tangled orchard is in danger of becoming a ghost. Perhaps she is a ghost already.

Herman, only too solid flesh, is being sick in the loo. Garlic.

Bea's eyes have adjusted to the darkness. The party guests who have left the garden through the same wicket gate, stand in murmuring couples and clusters or stroll on the beach. Standing at the edge of the loom of light from the house and the lanterned garden, Bea sees shapes take substance and holds her breath; then she realises that hunched, curled, squatting (watching?), the beach-bums, the sleepers, are gathered. (What do they want?) They are the colour, the shape and substance, of sand-dogs. She wonders what they want and as she watches she begins to make out a breathing bundle of rags here, a muzzle there, a snout here. No one else seems to have noticed them. Standing still at the circumference of the light as though it were a force field that held her, Bea says, or dreams she says: what do you want?

Someone speaks to her. When she next turns back they are gone. If they had ever been there.

'I'm sorry, what did you say?'

A couple she does not know have come up beside her.

'The lights,' says the woman she does not know. 'Aren't the lights pretty! Look, out at sea!'

There is something wrong with the lights. There is the lighthouse, then at the mouth of the bay pretty lights like a string of pearls or a seaside town. Others have noticed them, come out onto the beach.

'They're moving. It must be a ship.'

'They're not moving.'

'Are they moving?'

Finally, all the party has spilled onto the beach and everyone is watching the ocean. The party still goes on, they drink but don't talk so much: they are waiting to see what will happen. Herman, better now, joins Bea and she takes his hand. 'We'll go soon.' 'I wouldn't mind packing it in.' But they don't go. It's a lovely night.

Then just as it seems that nothing is going to happen, the lights go out, there is a sigh, a susurrus, and a red flower explodes in the air, hangs there, spills its petals. It is very beautiful.

Fireworks? No, a distress flare. There's another.

A ship on the rocks.

Almost everyone is ashamed of enjoying the spectacle. Harry rings the coastguard but the line is engaged. When the maroon goes off a couple reaching consummation in the boat-house learn the meaning of coitus interruptus. Merlyn is detached. Toby watches. Francine, flopped out in the hammock, shedding her little scarves, wonders where everyone has gone. Erin is distraught: Oh, Bea, how dreadful! On a night like this! How could it happen? Anything can happen anytime, says Jeannie, including shipwreck. When the maroon is fired Worthy Willings, like all good dogs, trots off to his basket.

5

WHEN EVERYONE WAKES the next day, after the party, the first thing they do is to look out of the window.

Bea has slept deeply, dreaming of a bay and a beach (neither of which, in the way of dreams, is exactly this bay and this beach); and across the corner of the dream there is a triangle of darkness, like a shadow on a photographic negative. So for a moment what she sees between sleeping and waking eerily corresponds to her dream – the pale morning promising heat, the empty bay, the lighthouse, and almost blocking the mouth of the bay that black shark shape.

'No – a whale,' says Mercy. She and Toby have sailed out in the lugger at daybreak to inspect the catastrophe. Mercy wears a tiny faded bikini: you could count her ribs, she hardly has breasts at all, her pelvic bones are sharp. She reminds Toby of pictures he has seen of victims of famine and someone he knew who died of heroin. Is that what Mercy's on? Some starvation trip? They say that in the last stages you see visions, but what's the use, Toby thinks, if you're dying? Toby's lust for Mercy is qualified. By a brotherly relationship. By her condition (is dying catching?). He wonders too if it is more difficult or easier to make love to someone you pity? If you wouldn't feel rather like a missionary? Come to think of it, he does feel like a missionary: he would, if he could, convert Mercy to life.

The first thing he should do, of course, if he is to save Mercy, is to remove her from that household. Everyone says that's what's the matter with Mercy and he supposes they must be right. He is lucky, the same people say, to be the child of a happy marriage, a *famously* happy mariage. He used to be proud of his parents for that when he was younger and he's proud now (officially), though there was a time when he was about sixteen that Toby felt like the child of film-stars, a bit freakish, embarrassed. At school everyone else had parents who were breaking up. Toby was the only one, apparently, who did not have two Christmases, two summer holidays, two lots of pocket money (with bonuses) and, in the case of re-marriage at least six doting grandparents. There was one boy who spent his summer holidays in one hemisphere, his winter vacations in another. Toby felt deprived.

Recently, he told Bea about this or some of it. They could talk about that sort of thing now, within limits. 'Poor old Timbo,' she said.

Toby could write a thesis on his parents' relationship: in this subject, he is a specialist. Some revisions may have to be made this summer.

He gybes the lugger. The breeze is always offshore in the morning. They are approaching the wreck, it is more clearly distinguishable. Figures can be seen moving gingerly on the upturned bows. Little tugs lie off. Small craft like their own are sailing or speeding towards the wreck – that looks like Jeannie Fisk in her Chris-Craft.

'It's a tanker,' says Toby. Then he wonders if visiting shipwrecks might not be a morbid pastime for Mercy. 'There's nothing much to see. Shall we go back?'

She shakes her head, she wants to go on (it is possible she is incurable). 'Will it break up?'

'Only if the wind changes and puts her on the rocks,' says Harry Fox, the practical one who knows such things. He stands, four-eyed, on the beach with binoculars with the Tylers, Erin Willings, and the Bonifaces. (Francine still sleeps off whatever it was she was on last night.) 'Then she might break her back.'

'How much oil?'

'Forty thousand tons. On the beach that would be. She was loaded. It's lucky she wasn't holed.'

What an irony, they think: oil, oil everywhere – yet since the shortage, hardly a drop to burn.

'Oh, those poor birds!' cries Erin.

'To hell with the birds,' says Jeannie. They're all drinking beer by her pool at midday. This is the white time when no wind blows. In an hour or two the onshore breeze will come up or not: anyway, in summer, it's never strong, more a hot breath as though someone had opened an oven door.

'You don't mind about birds?' asks Bea, interested (because her instinct is to preserve wild life, still Bea is not sentimental about it, nor does she expect everyone to share her views. A decade ago, Erin led marches to save the whale, handed out stickers, incited students and was distressed that Bea would not join in these games. The whale was not saved, anyway).

'There are things that matter more than the death of birds,' Jeannie answers.

Bea remembers the sea-swallow she and Timbo found dying, with oil in its feathers. If the tanker breaks up that small death will be multiplied a hundred, a thousand times. Suddenly, sadly, Bea realises she believes in evolution: that is, she feels it to be a force so powerful it cannot be resisted. She will still sit up all night with her birds. But now, watching them die by the ocean, or in the cage, she will regret her powerlessness to save them and at the same time think, well, that is how it must be. The bird – like individual goodness – is desirable but philosophically irrelevant: beyond the fact that it sings, eats nits and assists in pollination, its virtue cannot be defined. There is something dreadfully rational about evolutionary history.

Erin, stricken, pleads with Jeannie (always a pointless exercise): 'But Jeannie, it's a *moral* issue.'

'Moral shmoral,' snorts Jeannie. 'Where's the right and wrong?'

'Our responsibility!'

'Where's the ethic in responsibility?'

'Well, then – they're ecologically necessary. That's a fact.'

Jeannie drains her can. 'The ecology is collapsing – and that's an ecological fact. It is a fact that there is mercury in the shell-fish, strontium in the milk, the sea is poisoned, there are foxes in the city, there are mutated cows with toes that turn up, there are mutated sharks and there are no more whales. Everything, including man, is an endangered species. Either there are no wasps or giant wasps, plastics workers are dying, plutonium workers are dying, asbestos workers are dead, so is the American eagle and the wigeon's on the way out. When did you last see a butterfly?'

'But doesn't that *worry* you?'

'I don't worry about irreversible processes.'

'But what about the *children*!' In her distress, Erin looks like a child herself: a girl at a tutorial, leaning forward in the posture of learner who does not like the lesson. It's hard to imagine her teaching. What does she teach? Panic?

'They're an irreversible process too. They'll adjust. They have adjusted. We're the ones on the shelf.'

'Dinosaurs,' says Bea. She's drowsy from the late night and the beer. She wears wrap-around sunglasses and lies very still under her Martini umbrella. Her eyes dazzle. She sees Timbo wade through shaking heat to the watch-tower at the cliff-edge. He walks shoulders hunched, barefoot, hands in his pockets, head uncovered. 'Dinosaurs ruled the earth for 140 million years then the temperature changed and small mammals ate their food.'

'Come and get it,' says Jeannie. 'Tuna sandwich or tuna sandwich.'

They stay around the pool because everyone is tired this afternoon, after the party; and from here, without moving, they have a grandstand view of the catastrophe. The putative catastrophe – for nothing yet has happened, no lives have been lost. At least, they believe no lives have been lost. It's absurd, when they are so close to the accident, they cannot be sure; but no one has reason or inclination to go into town or down to the estuary landing, and reception for local radio and television is poor: it's something to do with the atmosphere, which garbles. They can get national news better, or satellite relays from another hemisphere. There is a marvellous picture of the African civil war (the *second* war, blacks v blacks) on Jeannie's portable Japanese television, and they slump by the afternoon pool, fighting sleep, half-watching the white reporter with a fly on his nose trying not to scratch his nose or throw up in a bush hospital where white nuns tend dying black babies with swollen bellies and old men's eyes. That's the white man's role in Africa now: witness and undertaker. Bea feels her belly cramp and remembers her dead children who were never born. Scraped from her uterus and washed down the drain or incinerated – she was encouraged to see them as menstrual errors and she has accepted, has adjusted, as would be expected of a sensible woman, yet she dreams of them still. Wonders, since they were wanted children, why her healthy sensible womb could not hold onto them.

There was so much blood.

Bea says: 'The birds may be the descendants of the dinosaurs. The skeletons are similar.' She walks through a museum she visited, characteristic of the northern protestant hemisphere she inhabits, white and pure. The attendants wore white rubber shoes, like nurses, the temperature was exactly controlled and the windows were sealed: otherwise the fossils would have turned to dust. Except for the rubbery pad of the attendants, there was a cathedral silence; which is not, of course entirely silent: after Bea had been standing for a while in the reptile room, she became aware of creakings and rustlings, the hum of the air-conditioning, the shuffle of feet in other rooms. Also, she realised that the reptile room was not as white as she had first imagined. There was something green about the light and the red of the fire-extinguisher shocked her. Although this was impossible, since petrification had taken place, she was faintly nauseated by the ossuary smell she had met before in mausoleums and in Tuscany in the graves. (It was possible that Bea had not got over her miscarriage as well as it appeared. At this time in her life, she saw connections between things that are unconnected and was dogged by images, as Francine was by her lobsters. Since she was not a novelist – even secret – Bea put down her mood to temporary insanity, which passed, as she knew it would. Once or twice in the years since, she has missed this mad eye and its useless insights.)

Bea says: 'There are many theories about dinosaurs.'

In the museum she started, like a child eating the bread and butter before the ice cream, with the smaller reptiles – lizards and turtles and snakes – saving for last the great Cretaceous Tyrannosaurus. Perfectly preserved and reconstructed (do not touch), he was the only one in this continent with every bony part intact, including the horn-like, tearing tooth. While she could feel more sisterly affection for the Iguanodon, as one plant-eater to another, it was to the flesh-eating Tyrannosaurus Bea always returned at this era. She never talked about her visits to the museum. When she left Timbo with a baby-sitter or a friend, she would say she was going shopping or to a class (this was in the city, of course); and then she would walk or take a cab (the buses made the journey awkward and bothered her for a while after her menstrual error) to walk up five white steps into the museum, show her student's card, open her handbag to confirm that she was not carrying a bomb, and cross the spongy soundless floor, by way of the smaller reptiles and the Iguanodon, to stand before Tyrannosaurus in horror and wonder at that great carnivorous warrior imprisoned in the cool, aseptic whiteness. This was probably the time when Bea rationalised her instinctive vegetarianism: carnivores seemed to her to lead a violent and precarious existence, dependent upon the flesh of others, threatened always by the whim of evolution. Once, when there was no one to leave him with, Bea took Timbo to the museum. No cabs were cruising their district and she felt that at five or six the walk would be too much for him, so they took two buses but a road was closed and they had to walk the last three hundred yards on this cold

November afternoon. Outside the museum there was a demo against some war, the demonstrators in their ratty anoraks with rabbit collars, their babies in back-packs, stamped to keep warm and hummed their slogan like a mantra. Inside the sealed silence of the museum Timbo, the least hysterical of children, cried when he saw Tyrannosaurus. He was over-tired, the demo had frightened him, Bea decided. As they came out onto the steps they saw that the world had changed. The snow fell and the demonstrators ceased their chanting, raised their faces to the white snow falling.

The reptiles perished at the end of the Cretaceous era, the birds originated in the Jurassic, which suggests that there might be something in Bea's theory about dinosaurs and birds.

Timbo caught a chill that afternoon and with the fever came nightmares about Tyrannosaurus. His child's breath smelled hot and sour. That, and the episode with the razor-shell, and his later somnambulism, were the only occasions when he gave them any serious anxiety (really, Bea and Herman told each other, they could hardly believe their luck with Timbo: superstitiously, Herman felt that their experience of child-rearing had been so far too good to be true. Everyone else seemed to have such problems – bed-wetting, epilepsy, dyslexia, thumb-sucking, just plain ghastliness: Tonio Boniface had a lot to answer for. Secretly, Herman could not quite credit that they would get off scot-free. Fearful of their luck, he almost *wanted* something not fatal to happen to Timbo, just to get it over with).

Bea never suffered from such fancies, or if she did, she never expressed them. But the afternoon of the demo and the blizzard marked for her, in a way, the end of an era. She got over her miscarriage, gave up her secret trysts with Tyranno-saurus, soon after stopped altogether going to the reptile room and concentrated on the smaller fossils.

When asked about that half-term holiday. Timbo beamed and told the Irish daily: my mother took me to see some dead bones.

*

Waking, Bea sees that the small blood-shot eye of the portable colour television by Jeannie's pool has finished with the war in Africa and gone on to cooking meat. A person is standing there in the uniform butcher's apron, cutting up part of a dead animal. (For a time there were not so many of these programmes: meat prices hit the roof and health faddery arrived – perhaps not coincidentally – at the same moment; in some quite grand houses it was no surprise to be served soya bean stew and brown rice along with vegetables home-grown in compost. A lot of people are still eating canned soya beans, but those who can afford it have lately largely gone back to meat: a kind of what-the-hell movement that probably means something or other. Bea and Timbo still actually prefer vegetables: they would never be faddists but they are fastidious.)

The person has cut up the meat. Now he throws it, along with a drunk-making marinade, into one of those mysterious crock pots that are all the rage and preserve the flavour; to the mixture the person adds chopped veg, more seasoning and a jug of reddish liquid.

'My God!' croaks Francine – who hobbled up the hill in time to shudder at the tuna sandwiches and collapse with a vodka and ice – 'that's *blood*!' This is the first time Francine has spoken that day. She is one of those lucky women a hangover makes sexier: her mouth is blurred, the skin beneath her eyes bruised, she has an air of translucence and abandon; she has been mistaken for a film-star she resembles.

Bea wonders whatever it is that Harry does to Francine in bed that could drive her to drink. Or is it that, drinking to escape her pursuant crustaceans, Francine has entered some terrible dream-world in which poor nice Harry makes upon her unnatural demands? Dreams are not to be discounted. We all have our reptile rooms.

The television suddenly dies on them. There is a lizard. The television cuts off the vampire cook. Harry fiddles with the transistor but he can get no news of the wreck. Bea sees a small greenery-yallery lizard cross one of the white slabs by the pool, then it freezes: fear, or the unforgiving light of mid-afternoon, has transfixed it. She imagines the dryness of its skin, the palpitation at the throat, the instinct to return to the lushness and the safety and the dark greenery of Jeannie's tropical wilderness. Worthy Willings, panting in the shade under Erin's lounger, sees the lizard and decides to co-exist – though he'll keep an eye on it, all the same.

They are in the hot eye of the afternoon. Herman, on rather than in the pool, precariously keeps his balance on the lilo as Merlyn crawls up and down, throwing up spray. Herman wears Bea's straw hat over his face and concentrates on stillness, malgré Merlyn; his hands serve as paddles but he uses them as little as possible, just a minimal adjustment of his displacement in the water (he has the feeling, like a child playing grandmother's footsteps, that if he keeps still he will escape the attention of death. He would if he could grow gills, stop breathing, sink greenly to the bottom of the pool and lie doggo, wise old carp). Whoever got sunstroke underwater?

There was a time when Herman found himself compulsively doodling on a memo slip on his briefcase on his lap in an aeroplane crossing the Alps, the word SILENCE written very small. That was the first occasion upon which Herman was aware of his Icarus problem. One moment he was doodling silence and glancing at the pretty shining peaks, the next the familiar mountains below had become ravenous fangs waiting to receive his falling body. Or the plane crashed and burned up or did not burn up but landed in snow and the passengers ate each other. Herman looked round for the person he would most like to eat or was most likely to be eaten by, he shammed sleep and from under half-closed lids scanned the cabin for hijackers and nuts with bombs in their handbags, really closed his eyes and listened for any irregularity in the engine hum as anxiously as he might attend the heartbeat of a dying relative (and when his own father was dying, he could not bear it, he went to Madrid). Herman worried about the pilot's tachycardia, the inefficiency of the ground crew who had failed to make fast a cargo door which would fly open and depressurise the aircraft – thus they would all be sucked from their seats and tossed into the thin air still carrying their plastic luncheon trays and briefcases and babies and bombs and handbags.

Herman doesn't know why he thinks so much about death – he knows it irritates Bea and he knows she knows he knows it irritates her. She's right, of course: tachycardia is hardly ever fatal. People have tricks for dealing with it – take a drink of cold water, bend down, touch your toes, and that leaping of the heart will be stilled. Herman is afraid his cranky heart – or, rather, his attitude to his cranky heart – may damage their famous marriage.

Herman does not think very much about their famous marriage. He is a little afraid that if he does think about it, it may go away. When he does think about it, he sees it as a third party – rather like a domestic animal that came to live with them many years ago and has become part of the family. Lately, he has speculated a little more upon the nature of this animal and wondered if one day it might turn and bite the hands that feed it; or simply walk out of the house and go away. He has no reason to think this, it seems improbable, but disaster – Herman has observed – comes frequently from a clear sky.

Herman dozes on the lilo on the beautiful blue pool and thinks of Bea: how she always delights him and can still astonish him. He thinks she spends too much of herself on other people. He is afraid that she might die, and without her, he would be desolate. He thinks of Timbo going and how it will be when they are left alone, once again after all these years, with their marriage: then they will find out what kind of dog it is.

One question Herman has never asked Bea: what were you doing in the museum that winter and why did you lie?

Merlyn leaps like Batman from the pool, showering them all with shining drops. Herman is capsized, his eyes sting with chlorine, for a moment he cannot see or breathe, his heart goes tickety tickety instead of tickety tock; Bea's straw sunhat sails away on a voyage to the deep end. Herman sets off after it and decides, let it go. He leaves the lilo and climbs from the pool. He sits on the edge of the pool to catch his breath. Bea is watching him, but from under the umbrella, behind the wrap-around sunglasses, he cannot read her face. He closes his eyes and remembers where his tablets are, in the little Victorian snuff-box Bea gave him last Christmas, in the bedroom, in his toilet bag with his shaving kit in the drawer of his bedside cabinet.

Harry calls. They're looking out to sea, pointing.

'Are you all right, Herman?'

'Absolutely all right, Erin.'

'Would you like a drink of water?'

'Truly, Erin, I'm fine.'

'You don't look quite right, Herman.'

'Absolutely fine. Tickety tockety.'

Merlyn has climbed to the top of the diving board. He stands there with his flat stomach. Merlyn's always tickety tockety.

'I think she moved,' Harry says, pointing to the wreck.

'I don't think she moved.'

'There, now! She moved.'

'Well, she's not moving now.'

'No, I don't think she moved.'

They flop back. Herman's all right now, ticking nicely. He feels exhilarated, daring. He sees Bea has been anxious after all, she is watching him with her glasses tipped up – Herman nods, she relaxes. Everyone turns to watch Merlyn on the high diving board. The sky is white. Merlyn stands against the white sky while the others below look up shading their eyes: he seems to stand there forever. The heat and the light have interfered in some way with time just as static interferes with local radio and television – time has become opaque like a glass of milky liquid, Merlyn will be forever poised to dive, Francine watching open-mouthed remembering her own fall from that same springboard.

Then as Merlyn arcs and executes a perfect dive Bea thinks: perhaps the dreadful thing has already happened, perhaps it was the wreck. Well, that's not her affair, though it's terrible, of course, about the birds.

'What will they do about the wreck?' she asks Harry Fox.

Harry shrugs. 'Try to float her at high water?' He looks worried but then Harry Fox often looks worried. He's a nuts and bolts man of divine longings, who would, if he could, make do and mend on a universal scale. Poor Harry, thinks Bea, he must be constantly distressed by ineptitudes he is powerless to heal. The top of his bald head is freckled and he has ginger tufts of hair on his chest, short square fingers. 'The trouble is we're coming up to high spring tides – the highest for years.'

'Isn't that good?'

'If they get her off. If not, it's bad. Did you know, Bea,' – Harry's tone is confidential and solemn – 'this country is sinking a foot every hundred years? And the sea is rising?'

'No, I didn't know that.' Bea can never tease Harry. There is something touching about him.

Jeannie Fisk has no such scruples. 'Take to the lifeboats!'

'Oh, it will be a very gradual process,' says Harry.

Entering the water, Merlyn makes no splash. The water simply opens to receive him. He does not surface but swims around underwater. Perhaps he is evolving, growing gills, and will step out laconically web-footed. Bea sees that the lizard is still there on the baking slab: the reptile was the first creature to step ashore from the primeval sludge, to make its way to Jeannie's tropical garden where a hose plays day and night. The children are not supposed to go there alone because of the little snakes.

No one speaks. Even under their parasols, behind their sun-cream and dark glasses, with their cool minty drinks, they are struck dumb by heat. On the hinterland there are puffs of smoke, spontaneous combustion or some tripper's cigarette. The wrecked ship becomes a shaking phantasm – it could go down and they'd never notice. It may never have been there.

Bird-boned Mercy thinks she is too fat.
Bea thinks: if the world ends, it could be by this pool.

Toby sits on the cliff-edge below the watchtower. From here the sea looks so bland and innocent. Polluted? Who? Me? The horseshoe bay perfectly contains the picture-book sea, the small motor craft, the becalmed sailing boats. The lighthouse stands guard as it always has (the fact that it has been automated has nothing to do with last night's disaster: there has been no malfunction). Toby remembers cutting his foot once on a razor-shell on the lighthouse island – that was the very first time he can actually recall the injustice of unnecessary pain. What had he done to the razor-shell? That was what really shocked him: he'd learned already or been taught the perils of the city but it had never occurred to him that nature too might be hostile. At that age (five? six?) he hadn't expressed his disillusionment in these terms, of course, but for a while he was windy of the beach. Fear had entered into him.

About the same time his mother took him to the reptile room in the museum. Toby doesn't remember much about that, but he does remember he was ill in winter and in his dreams he was chased around the beach by a carnivorous dinosaur.

When he was a little older – Bea knows nothing about this – Toby had fantasies about meeting and killing the monster Tyrannosaurus. That was when he believed in the joy of mortal combat. He's grown out of that now, but he still suspects the old meat-eater may be around somewhere.

Toby thinks he'd like to swim out to the lighthouse island this summer – he's never done that. He makes a kind of vow: if he loses his virginity this summer, he'll swim to the lighthouse island. He sits, knees up under his chin, half-closes his eyes, then shuts them – as he did as a child, when he was a wizard and could make the world disappear. Ho! You are in my power. You are all gone! In his mind – in a very secret, private part of his mind – the tanker blows up: that would be something happening! Someone's calling. Mercy? There is a scent of some very dry herb, like sage or rosemary.

Toby opens his eyes.

The world remains.

6

WHO WILL GIVE the next party, Jeannie or the Tylers? Will Mercy die or will she run away to be a terrorist, or will Toby save her? Will Merlyn get Erin with an axe? Will the tanker break up?

Anything can happen any time, as Jeannie says, including shipwreck.

Everyone has a history, thinks Bea, and that's a dangerous cargo – people talk about accidents but there is no such thing, no act outside history. She should know. People are always bringing her their histories and dumping them on her lap as though they could be rid of them that way. Sometimes they do not tell her the truth, she knows; but that lying is in itself a truth about them, she knows that too.

Once she met a woman on a train who said she had been in the concentration camps and barely avoided the ovens (this was not possible: the woman could not have been more than thirty). The next week she saw the woman's picture in the paper: she had poured petrol over herself and burned to death. That was no accident.

Bea knows too much about almost everyone here, with the possible exception of her own son, Timbo. Erin has confided in her about Merlyn, Merlyn about Erin, Merlyn and Erin about Mercy. Mercy used to confide in her, but not lately.

The men are all up to something or other, to do with fish or boats, so the women are left to each other's mercy.

Erin sits on the beach, painting the view of the bay.

She wears a loose blue cotton smock and a floppy sunhat. She paints like a child – with immense concentration, her tongue stuck out, foreground before background: a couple of beach dogs playing, a child with a ball, a gay little yacht, then the headland, the lighthouse, the sea, the sky. Bea loves Erin's paintings. There is an innocence about them, a joyousness, something unguarded that Erin has, against odds, preserved intact.

Erin sucks the handle of her brush. She cannot decide whether to include the crippled tanker.

'The trouble is, it's there.'

Bea looks up from her book. 'But it wasn't a week ago and it might not be tomorrow. You're not a photographer.'

Erin frowns. She paints in the tanker. It looks like a shark, sleek and menacing, or a shadow. Now it's a sad picture.

The women meet on Francine Fox's balcony. Merry plays in the sand-pit below with the little Foxes. Jeannie brings vodka, which is coals to Newcastle. No one has asked Betty Boniface. No one ever asks Betty Boniface, except for Tonio's sake.

Francine brings out cocktail onions, gherkins and cheese sections. The women drink, lie in the shadow or sun themselves. They are pleased with each other, there is the camaraderie of being women, something powerful among old friends. At some point, for all of them, their histories have overlapped, they are soldiers seasoned by the same campaigns.

Also, they are a little tipsy, while the men fish.

Jeannie lays down that Mercy won't eat because she doesn't want to be a woman and who can blame her?

Only Jeannie would have been tactless enough to bring up Mercy in front of Erin. Only Erin would have been idiotic enough to respond. Her eyes shine dangerously, they may overflow.

'Oh, Jeannie, I never thought of that!'

'Well, it's obvious, isn't it. Look at us.'

Bea doesn't approve of this conversation. She has had the sense that something bad may happen this summer, but does not believe it has anything to do with being female. On the whole, she enjoys being a woman. She thinks women are stronger, anyway – with all their woes, they have the gift of survival. She has never, for instance, met a woman with cardiac neurosis. Women can do terrible things and get away with them.

For example: no one knows and Bea will probably never tell anyone, that the year of the visits to the reptile room, she had an affair with a palaeontologist specialising in reptiles (that is how she knows so much about dinosaurs). Because she is a sensible woman, and regards that period of her life as a time of unreason, she has always considered the indiscretion with Paul Harbinger as irrelevant to her history and, in particular, to the famous history of her marriage. For the same reason, she never felt the need to confess to Herman. In fact, she has virtually forgotten it herself – when it was over, it was over, Bea simply took a deep breath and walked out into the snow – and she is surprised to be remembering it now. Affronted.

She saw him in the museum, of course, and then they met in the coffee-shop (Bea cannot remember anything they said on that occasion, though she can see it, as a conversation observed underwater). They probably talked about reptiles and one day carried on talking, up the stairs from the basement coffee-shop, through the foyer, out down the steps and round the corner to his small, astonishingly over-heated room: like stepping out of a refrigerator into a South American swamp.

There might have been crocodiles.

That made it all the more exciting, to lie under the skinny boy with orange hair she could twist in her fingers, and pale eyelashes, sweating to death while the snow fell down outside.

'Harbinger, What sort of a name is that? It sounds like doom.'

Harbinger was young to be an expert on reptiles. He made love very noisily with strange astonished cries, unlike Herman, who chatted or was silent or made pleased, satisfied grunts, like a man going home after a hard day and shutting the door behind him.

Bea and Harbinger did all kinds of amazing things: they licked one another's faces, and other parts. Bea thought perhaps this was the affair she did not have before marriage, also the student days that marriage cut off.

'I love you,' said Harbinger, sweating, 'I love making love to you,' he gasped. Afterwards, they sat wrapped in Red Indian blankets while he read her his thesis.

'I don't think,' said Bea, 'that I'm very stable at the moment.'

Harbinger didn't hear her. He talked about himself, he found himself very interesting, and so, for a time, did she. Then Harbinger wanted her to grow her hair and leave her husband. When Bea said no, she felt as though she had kicked a gerbil (which Harbinger resembled). He looked breakable. He huddled by his paraffin heater clutching his Indian rug around him, shivering as if someone had forgotten to feed him. I'm sorry, Paul, said Bea. He seemed young but that was nearly fifteen years ago, so there couldn't have been much in their ages. She felt sad leaving him and would have liked to make some gesture, but as she reached to touch him, Harbinger hissed: leave me alone, you're mad. He even followed her to the door and shouted after her down the stairs, over the banister: 'There's something crazy inside you! I hope you freeze in hell! You're a monster, a mad, crazy woman!' Bea took a deep breath and walked out into the snow. That was the winter she took Timbo to the museum.

Now she comes to think about it, Timbo looks a little like Harbinger at that age. Though, unlike Harbinger, he doesn't march in demos. There are few demos to march in nowadays. But he has the same bird-boned gawkish look (surely deceptive) of some starveling creature too proud to accept scraps.

*

Worthy Willings prefers the company of women. Francine Fox tries to feed him cheese sections and he thumps his tail, refusing politely. Cheese gives him constipation.

Paul Harbinger's dead now. He went missing in some swamp country and was believed to have been crucified by a tribe that has since become extinct. Two or three times in the years between Bea thought she caught a glimpse of him in the street, and ran after him, but it was always someone younger, about Timbo's age now.

Women are survivors.

Bea's mother, for instance, was a survivor: a wiry, sharp woman, with none of her daughter's charity, who spent twenty years dying and despised death, as though it were some gatecrasher she had not invited to dinner, almost to the end. Bea realises now that she never cared much for her mother, Sarah – which made her dying, in a way, even more of an ordeal – though she came to admire her defiance.

The other side of Sarah's proud courage was a blinkered refusal to adapt to change: whether to the cancer in her body or to the way of the world. She belonged, perhaps, to the last generation that knew it was right.

Bea sees her mother on her knees on a rubber kneeling mat, attacking some disorderly plant in her garden with secateurs. Looking up in her bright garden to say: they tell me I must stay in for tests, her mouth turned down. No, that was the hospital: Sarah sitting up in bed reading C. P. Snow, looking like a cross child who has been kept from a party.

To witness – that is perhaps the least you can do for any death. Bea wondered through her mother's dying if Harbinger had not been right, if she might be some kind of monster, for she felt more than anything, embarrassed (as if she had found Sarah making love, or peeing in the street): so Bea the undutiful daughter sat every afternoon for an hour by Sarah's bed reading, later reading aloud for Sarah; asked the doctors the right desolate questions and hardly slept at night waiting for the telephone to call her out, to see Sarah off. She did witness.

She doesn't like being drugged, Bea remembers telling the doctors.

Once, when Bea thought her to be dozing, her mother said: you have time for everyone in the world but me.

Bea has always been known for her kindness. Charity does not often begin at home.

To her mother Bea said finally, as gently as she could, they are only trying to help you, to save you pain. But almost to the end Sarah fought the drugs – there was a gleam in her eye that said: I will live, I *will* live. Such tenacity: the image of the child again, who refuses to go to bed. And like a tired child, Sarah was fractious, complaining of the mushy nursery food (once actually knocking the bowl from Bea's hand), that she was hot, that she was cold, that the nurses were brutal and the doctors ignorant. Her room reminded Bea of the museum – the same whiteness, sealed windows, rubber-soled attendants: and in this reptile room images gathered and cloyed, the poinsettia at the foot of the bed seemed to bleed, there was the sweet and meaty scent of Jeannie's tropical garden.

After the dying, the death was not so much. At some point in the terminal coma Sarah simply ceased to breathe, while Bea slept on the cot beside her bed. Later, washed and laid out, her cheeks stuffed with cotton wool, Sarah seemed in the rictus of death to have recaptured her ferocity. She was alarming and slightly magnificent. Bea, a little crazy with exhaustion, saw her mother on show in a room like this: an admirable relic, frightening children.

One of the women on the Foxes' balcony says: let's take the children to fossil beach.

'Too hot.'

'Who'll give the next party?'

As long as she doesn't think about Mercy, Erin among women can be more or less happy.

'But Jeannie,' she persists, 'what's so awful about being a woman?'

'Not being a man,' says Jeannie. 'Oh, what the hell.'

Bea pretends to doze. Francine once danced on the table with a carnation in her teeth. Everything seems to have happened once. Friends enquire tenderly of one another: have you made your will? It's this age we are, and the times.

When Bea was at her mother's deathbed and Herman was in Madrid, and Herman's father was dying, Timbo had to cope with his grandfather. A raw way to be thrust into your first experience of death, yet miraculously he seemed to emerge unscathed. Perhaps at that age death is not a disaster? Or everything then is assimilable and equal, a broken skateboard or a death? No, not for Timbo, Bea felt; he would never have it so easy.

Herman came home from Madrid, but immediately contracted shingles, then there was the trouble with his heart (or his head), so Timbo had to keep up the deathwatch.

When it was all over Bea made a point of thanking him.

Timbo looked puzzled. 'I didn't mind.'

And he really didn't, that was the astonishing thing. Sometimes at that era in his life Bea worried that Timbo seemed too ready – *unnaturally* ready – to assume adult responsibilities. He had been a grave child. Was he turning into a grave adult, skipping adolescence? (Bea once confessed to Jeannie that she almost wanted to find that Timbo had been drinking too much or smoking – everyone had to do something silly at some point before they woke up middle-aged. 'Does he have a sex life?' asked Jeannie. 'If he doesn't have a sex life he ought to be masturbating.')

Of course, Timbo did love his grandfather. There had been the ease between the very old and the very young speaking across a generation. More than a companionship, there was an alliance, an exclusive relationship. Who – when you came to think about it – was, accordingly, better fitted to attend the old man's death? Perhaps, Bea thinks sometimes, we try too hard to protect our children from acquaintance with death? What is it, after all, but another fact of life?

If we spoke of death every day of our lives, it might lose its magic. But what a life. Of course, that was unthinkable, who could live that way? (Herman does).

Toby has a secret life, of which Bea knows nothing; he has always had this – even when he was very young, and so open and sweet. His mind – she has come to realise only lately – is a well fortified castle to which she is, from time to time, a privileged visitor. There may even be dungeons. There are certainly ghosts.

When he was about seven Bea took Timbo, against her inclination, to the zoo (because all his friends had been and he hadn't, and he asked to go). It was winter, in the city, a bright, sharp day, all the cages rimed with frost and the artificial lake half frozen over. Bea remembers how a cold mist cleared about three, just as they arrived, and the weak sun fired into gold the windows of the tower blocks that surround the zoo park: from the empty park it was a vision of some lost civilisation, its peopleless monuments preserved.

The zoo was well designed. Wherever possible bars had been avoided and instead pits prevented escape. Really, it hardly looked like a prison at all – so spacious were the living quarters. All the animals and birds seemed healthy and there were several rare species hardly seen in the wild any more. Bea felt happier about them – if they had not been here, they would be on the way to extinction.

At first Timbo ran ahead. He wore a red anorak – almost the only spot of colour in the white zoo – but then he began to drag his feet and Bea to suspect that the zoo had not been such a brilliant idea after all. For a normally even-tempered child, he was being quite perverse. Then the sun went down and they left the zoo park only just in time before the gates were locked.

That summer at the beach-house Timbo opened the door of the hospital cage to let out a convalescent tern. A cat got in and killed it. Bea explained: 'You see, it couldn't have survived in any case, with a broken wing, not on its own. And cats kill birds, it's natural.' Timbo looked at his mother as though she had just attempted to justify genocide. With uncharacteristic mawkishness, he insisted on giving the tern a full state funeral. A grave was dug above the high-water mark, the remains of the bird placed in a cat-proof box, lowered into the sand, covered, and a cairn of pebbles set at the head. Timbo and Mercy did it together, very solemnly. That year there was a freak spring tide and the little monument was washed away.

The women have stopped talking for the moment, even Erin. Francine Fox is painting her toenails blood red. Bea opens her eyes and suddenly she wants to tell someone about Harbinger, but she won't. Or one day she might tell Jeannie.

There is something comfortable between the women this afternoon, as though, in their various postures of happy exhaustion, a silken and magical thread runs between their fingers, connecting them.

Erin is squatting in the sandpit with the children. Bea looks down at her and at that moment Erin looks up and smiles. Jeannie is snoring with her mouth open. Francine finishes the last toenail, screws up the bottle, sighs and lies back. How beautiful she is.

Crazy. But not dumb, or not as dumb as Jeannie thinks.

Bea thinks she would like to go home and do something sensible. Make bread. Cook. Spend a long time, an hour at least, preparing a recipe that tasted simple but demanded a great deal of chopping modest ingredients – onion, for instance – very finely. Such casseroles – they are mostly casseroles – Bea always thinks of, with some mockery, as her virtuous dishes. She cooks like this when she is in need of grace. It's difficult at the beach-house because here she works mostly from the freezer, but it can be done. When Herman was away and Timbo was younger, he used to watch fascinated as his mother performed this ceremony. It became a joke between them: my mother's being a Good Woman.

Bea cooks like this. Other women knit or write novels or become alcoholics. Bea has thought more than once, it's the luck of the draw, it could go any way, she does not particularly admire herself. In the same way she happens to collect fossils while Jeannie collects young lovers.

Francine collects vodka empties. Some people would say that was the most important fact about her but Bea would disagree because she believes in history and there were all those years of Francine's life before she met lobsters and took up vodka; and no one fact is the most important fact about anyone.

For instance, it matters also that Francine is beautiful. The day Bea found her drunk, sent the little Foxes round to Erin and sat reading Harry's *New Technology*, waiting for Francine to wake up, Francine told her that when she was very young she wanted to be clever, not beautiful. But she was supposed to be a pretty little girl, and her mother dressed her accordingly.

'She permed my hair when I was six,' Francine confessed. 'Can you *imagine* that Bea? I felt like a doll. So that's what I became. And when I was old enough, there I was, a doll in a box and all men wanted to do was rape me. Harry raped me.' Francine, only just out of her blind, talked with her face turned away, her hand half-covering her mouth, smoking and smoking. And on and on she talked. 'A woman gets used to rape, don't you think, Bea? I think that, I don't think it's Harry's fault, it's mine, I blame myself, I don't even blame my mother.' The idea of nice, sensible Harry raping anyone was so fantastic Bea couldn't credit it – yet other people's marriages, other people's lives, were fantastic beyond belief: if Bea had learned nothing else, she'd learned that. She'd learned too that anyone in trouble will do their best to present themselves as innocent victims. When they finally say I blame myself, perhaps they are getting somewhere. So she listened and listened, and Francine talked, concluding finally: 'Bless you, Bea. You're a good listener.' Something else Bea had discovered was that the role of confessor is a dubious one, it can turn against you. People tell you too much and they can never forgive you for that (except for Erin, who forgives everyone everything). Bea can never understand why people tell her so much: she does not think of herself as a particularly kindly person nor even wise (a monster, Harbinger said, a crazy monster).

She did ask Francine: 'If Harry raped you, why on earth did you marry him?'

Francine lay back on the sofa, her tangled long dark hair spread, her gaze turned to the ceiling.

'But that's the *point*, Bea,' she wailed, 'I *want* to be raped! That's why I blame myself.'

Bea wondered if Merlyn Willings raped Francine – he seemed better cut out for the role than Harry. Perhaps that was the trouble? Harry didn't rape Francine enough?

The heart of the matter was that Francine was unhappy, for whatever reason. Bea realised that they were not talking about rape at all. They were talking about victims.

There are the men, coming up the beach. They have caught fish. The women are on the balcony, the men start up the beach carrying their catch. Between them the beach-dogs play and scrap, then scatter as the men approach but they do not go far away. Someone – Merlyn? – throws them a fish. A bloody fight ensues – the winner runs yelping off but he won't keep the fish long. Those dogs will eat anything: fish, rats, cats. Every night there's a dustbin raid. And still they're all ribs and teeth. Jeannie Fisk says they're a rabies hazard – she wants to shoot them. She might too.

There is the ghost of a growl from Worthy, he's keeping an eye on those wild dogs.

The approach of the men breaks the spell among the women.

Francine yawns: 'Who's giving the next party then?'

It isn't much of a catch. Toby hands his mother a mackerel.

It's very pretty, shiny blue and pink, but what can you do with one fish? They give it to the cat, who leaves the head, spine and eyes in Bea and Herman's bed. A tribute? A threat?

7

THE TYLERS WILL give the next party.

It is getting towards midsummer. Nothing now but an electrical storm will slake the dry earth. So far there has been only one clap of thunder out of a clear blue sky.

The summer people are lucky, of course, to be here by the ocean. They are not spoiled children, they appreciate their fortune and congratulate each other daily not to be elsewhere. Bea tries to telephone the Catarullas, who have taken their house for the summer, but there is a fault on the line. She is not sorry to be cut off from the city.

Merlyn gets up at six in the cool of the day to write his secret novel. Rat-a-tat-tat he goes, one-fingered, torn between doubt and triumph. One moment he is writing a perfect book, the next the novel – the bourgeois novel in particular – is dead. He will never finish his secret novel and secretly, he knows this. Even Merlyn Willings has that core of terror and wonder that makes him human, makes him doubt. Makes him write and makes him want to run away with Francine into a book. He's not as awful as he seems. No one is. He wants Merry to wake up, so that he can play with his daughter on the beach.

The novelist is lonely with his percolating coffee in the green-shaded house where not a foot falls yet but his on the quiet stone floors. WILL SOMEONE PLEASE WAKE UP?

Toby wakes about the same time and lies in his solitary bunk-bed in the room that was, he knows, designed to recall vaguely a ship's cabin. He's always felt that he should have appreciated this more but he has never quite managed to say straight out to his mother or his father: 'Thank you for designing my bedroom to look like a ship's cabin.' He was very young when they first had the beach-house so it seems to Toby that one day he just woke up and found that his room resembled a ship's cabin. At that age he probably thought that it was perfectly normal to have a room like this. Then for a while he wondered if they expected him to be a sailor. By the time he realised that his parents' motives had been pure and he was quite lucky to have such an unusual room, Toby felt it was too late to say anything: as ridiculous in a way as thanking them for his fourth birthday party, or for having him at all.

Well, that had been quite a triumph, he now grasped, that he should have been born, bearing in mind his mother's miscarriages. A triumph for her womb or for his tenacity, he had no idea. In fact, when you came to think about it, birth was very dodgy. To have been conceived at all a miracle. When they had sex classes at school, years ago, Toby remembers at the tender age of eight or so, finding the information neither smutty nor embarrassing (a little irrelevant, in fact, as his mind was more on skateboards at the time than procreation). Yet astonishing, from the sperm's point of view – this heroic battle of the tadpoles. Why had he won, he wondered? He was no hero. He discussed the matter with Tike Willings (always precociously informed on such matters) but all even Tike could offer was: 'Well, you're a good swimmer.'

'But plenty of people can't swim.'

'Maybe they could before they were born and they've forgotten.'

'You never forget. It's like riding a bike.'

Tike, lying in the upper bunk in the ship's cabin bedroom, yawned.

He was an ends man. Means bored him.

Before Worthy, Toby recalls, the Willingses had a bitch. Erin wouldn't have her spayed, so she was often pregnant (she might have been Worthy's mother, but Toby can't remember that). Of indeterminate breed, she was no beauty and after her first litter she never regained her figure: her dugs hung down permanently.

Her name was Charity, and she was certainly generous in her favours. Though plain (beagle's legs on spaniel's body), Charity had sex appeal. When she came on heat, there was no holding her. Toby heard his mother tell his father that she suspected Erin of letting her out. If Erin hadn't let her out, she'd probably have broken down the door.

One summer afternoon, when the adults were off in town or somewhere, Tike appeared on the Tylers' porch. He looked pleased with himself.

'Got something to show you.'

'What?'

'Wait and see.

'Where?'

'In our shed. You'd better hurry.'

Toby had no idea what to expect, but he didn't much care for Tike in this mood. When they got to the broken-down boatshed by the Willingses' hard, Tike put his finger to his lips and made Toby kneel by a crack in the boards. There, curled on an old sail bag, Charity was making strange whimpering noises.

'Is she ill? Shouldn't we help her?'

Tike shook his head. 'She's pupping.'

It was horrible, it was incredible, as four weird little blood-soaked bodies, like blind rats, emerged from Charity. At first Charity lay panting, then she turned to lick them. Toby was sure they were dead. He felt sick. He walked down to the edge of the sea and flung pebbles. That afternoon he and Tike had a fight – one of those tussles that are necessary between boys, half a kind of love, half war: but this time Toby wanted to hurt his friend, and he did not know why. When his mother asked him what he had done that afternoon he shrugged. She had the sense not to press it – his mother was a sensible woman. For Toby this was an unlooked-for experience of violence, a confirmation that old Tyrannosaurus was still around, somewhere, always. You could run but you'd never escape him. Not on your life.

In having him, had Bea suffered as dreadfully as Charity? Toby worried about this for at least twenty-four hours. He went on quarrelling with Tike Willings for a week – or, rather, he refused to play with him and refused to explain why. Bea didn't pester, she never did, but she was clearly baffled and a little worried. It didn't seem *natural* for a boy Toby's age not to go around with a playmate when a playmate was available. Instead, Toby seemed to be spending the whole day in his room, or he went off on mysterious solitary treks into the hinterland (not fossil beach, because he might meet Tike there).

Then one morning Tike turned up as they were having breakfast on the porch. He stood with his hands in his pockets, kicking the shingle.

'We're going on a picnic. Want to come?'

'All right,' said Toby, as though nothing had happened. The estrangement was over as mysteriously as it had begun.

For many years Toby, Mercy and Tike went around together. Mercy was almost as good as a boy in those days. She swam, sailed, climbed trees, made dens, and for a while both Toby and Tike were hopeful that she might not turn into a female at all. When they became academically interested in the anatomy of the opposite sex she stripped off obligingly one day at the Willings's when everyone was out. Though there was very little to see (her breasts were hardly formed), Toby was astonished by the softness of her flesh – naked, sturdy brown-legged Mercy was as vulnerable as an unpeeled mollusc. In the shaded bathroom, her skin had a green watery tinge, seemed to waver. Toby was awestruck. When Tike suggested they should strip off too, Toby refused. He wasn't sure when he thought about it if his scruples had something to do with sin or with doubts about his own body – if it was as good as anyone else's. He felt foolish. After all, it was only a year or two since he'd taken *baths* with Mercy. And his parents had never loaded him with that sort of prohibition (though they didn't do it themselves, they belonged to the kind of people that walked around naked in front of their children and never locked the bathroom). Maybe he simply decided that he'd had enough revelations for one day.

Then he thought it might have been different if Tike hadn't been there. There was something about his friend's worldly, knowing presence that put Toby off (it still does). Tike had seen a friend of his mother's stark naked through a thin shower curtain when he was six. He knew the interesting bits in the Bible. He taught Toby to masturbate.

After the bathroom strip-show things went back to normal for a while, then, when they were all about eleven, Mercy became thin and was no use as a boy at all. She'd spend hours with Bea with the fossils or the birds and otherwise seemed to prefer to be by herself. She and Tike quarrelled a lot. She was still nice enough to Toby but he was changing too, of course, and there was a distance between them. Across this area of demarcation they watched one another, waiting to see what would happen. At this time, Toby noticed, Mercy really seemed to suffer from the battletorn Willings household. It was about then she began to walk with a stoop, as though ducking missiles. She became protective of Erin. The only thing she ever said to Toby about this was: 'My mother's not very good at living. I mean, she doesn't know how it works – like not knowing how to ride a bike.'

Around the same time – he must have been thirteen, Mercy fourteen – Toby became a nightwalker. Once he woke up on the Willings's doorstep, once in Bea's hospital cage on the lawn. Bea didn't fuss but she must have been worried. For once she was quite sharp with Erin, who had all kinds of theories. They should send Toby to an analyst. They should buy him a pet.

'Erin, for heaven's sake!'

Jeannie Fisk said they should take him to a brothel.

'It's perfectly normal in Latin countries.'

'This is not a Latin country. I doubt if there are any brothels.'

115

'I didn't mean you, Bea. I meant Herman.'

'Can you *imagine* Herman? Honestly, Timbo's just pu-bescent – everyone goes through that.'

'Sometimes I think, Bea, you're very hard,' said Erin bravely. 'We can't all be as strong as you.'

(You're a monster, Harbinger said.)

Erin, of course, immediately repented. How could she do otherwise? Bea had been so kind to her, she was the best of friends. Erin could have bitten off her tongue.

'It doesn't matter, Erin, really.'

'But it does! Anyhow,' concluded Erin in a small voice, 'you must be the only one of us who doesn't have to worry about her children. Toby will be fine, I'm sure.'

Then, between Erin, Francine and Betty Boniface, there began one of those wailing conversations women have about the awfulness of their children. Even the most intelligent women, Bea had noticed, did this; in fact, the better educated they were, the more they seemed to wail. Bea could not join this curious female fellowship for the simple reason that she never found Timbo awful.

Yet as an only child he should, by all the rules, have been frightful.

Toby was fine. His somnambulism lasted only a month, then it stopped. What he did (without Bea's knowledge) was to tie his ankle with a piece of thread to the post at the bottom of his bunk bed, so when he tried to step out, he woke.

Toby realised at about four that he was an only child. He immediately invented an imaginary companion called Timbo. At first, when he said 'Timbo wants ice-cream' or 'Timbo is cross', his parents thought he was talking about himself – hence the nickname stuck, long after Bea and Herman had come to accept the invisible fourth person who demanded an extra plate at table (Bea stopped short of actually feeding it); long after this uninvited guest had departed forever.

Then briefly Toby desperately wanted a brother or sister. Later he realised he had been lucky to have been born at all and gave up such complaints, though in his mind there still lay curled that dream-sibling. Which explains some complications in his relationship with Mercy. He loved her. The point was *how* did he love her? If she were his dream-sister, then the thoughts he had about her sometimes made him some kind of mad incestuous rapist. How do you make love to a girl you've had baths with? Shared the same plastic duck?

One time Bea confessed to Toby that after the miscarriages she had seriously considered adopting (so it is not quite true that she never worried about him being the only one). She didn't tell him this until he was about fifteen.

'Well, of course,' she said, as they drove along the coast-road one day (they had some of their best conversations in cars), 'I felt it might be bad for you, being an only child. People kept telling me, and I laughed at them. But I suppose it did bother me a bit.'

'It's never bothered me at all,' said Toby. He lounged comfortably in his seat. He always felt happy in a car with his mother: Bea was a good, crisp driver, even though she had to sit on a cushion to reach the wheel. His father drove fast and erratically, as though the road were mined (perhaps it was as well Herman was not an airline pilot).

'Truly?'

'Oh well, just for a while, when I was small. Maybe a little.' He grinned and Bea smiled back at him from the driving mirror. 'Why didn't you? Adopt, I mean.'

'I don't really know, It was one of those ideas. Perhaps your father wasn't keen. Then I saw you were all right. Well, you've only got to look at the Bonifaces, the Willingses, the Foxes. But for a couple of years I did feel a freak. People are still peculiar about that sort of thing. Then I used to reply, this was my contribution to zero population growth.'

'I'm glad you didn't.'

Bea thought, is he being truthful or courteous? She drove on. They stopped at the headland, drew off the road and sat looking out at the sea and the lighthouse island and the ocean beyond, bland and teeming. Not half so fruitful though, as it used to be.

She lit a cigarette and glanced at Toby sprawled beside her: the long legs, skinny wrists, strong arms, hands still not quite finished, and thought how he was so entirely himself, how he was becoming mysterious – with the gentlest smile, closing one little door against her, after another. And at the same time – how incredible! I made him. These years though, not birth, are the true moments of parturition.

'Oh well,' she said, like a sigh, as though she had delivered herself of something quite profound.

At the same time Toby wakes in his ship's-cabin-bedroom, Mercy is sitting in her pretty attic room under the eaves of the Willings's house, trying to write an essay on Virginia Woolf for her Landmarks of Literature course. Below her the house is stirring. She does not go downstairs because she doesn't want breakfast or a wrangle about breakfast; also, she is putting off as long as possible the moment when she will have to assume parental responsibility for her mother and father. Her mother in particular. She is afraid that her father may kill her mother or her mother may kill herself. Ten years ago Mercy used to sit in this room with her hands over her ears, while the battle raged below. Once she actually hid the carving knife, Erin's pills and Merlyn's axe. She knows that Toby thinks she should go away, for her own sake; but for Erin's sake, how can she?

Mercy pushes back the flop of hair over her forehead and writes in a sloping hand: "Virginia Woolf removed the constraints of naturalism from the English novel." Having done this, Mrs W. went down to the river and walked in. Well, at least she had no daughter.

Mercy does not wish to die, she simply desires to become invisible.

A new factor has been added this summer: she wishes that Toby could accompany her into invisibility. Pushing aside Virginia, Mercy thinks about Toby. She thinks no further than the fact that she would like to see him today, hopes she will. Suddenly, Mercy feels hungry.

Since the weather got hotter Worthy Willings has more or less adopted the Tylers. He returns at night politely to his own basket, but each morning before the sun becomes too brazen he drinks from his bowl and trots along the beach. The only drawback about the Tylers is their terrible cat: prudently, Worthy does his best to avoid it but if it's around he dozes with one eye open. He spends most of the day sitting in the shade on the porch, often under Bea's wicker chair. Towards the middle of the day he falls into a deep slumber. In his old age Worthy's dream life has become extraordinarily vivid, rich and exhausting. When Bea is sitting with him she protects his sleep. He whines, twitches and sometimes he thumps his tail.

To Bea there has been something dream-like about this whole summer so far – as though they were playing out a parable in an imagined country of shifting realities. The air shakes. She feels insubstantial. Her cool fossils do not always console her. She needs specifics, something to anchor her to the earth, like gardening. She is sure she remembers growing roses and marigolds; now the climate here has become so extreme no one but Jeannie with her tropical folly could coax more than sea-lavender and thrift from these sand and salt-lashed gardens. Seeking the virtue of occupation, Bea agrees they will give the next party and sits on the porch making lists.

To Herman she says: 'I think a beach party, don't you? Like the old days – on the island. If the tanker hasn't broken up.'

'Mmm.'

They both squint, shading their eyes to see the tanker – as do all the beach people, as a matter of course, several times a day; though no longer so obsessively – the tanker has become part of their lives, like a detached retina it casts a shadow over a corner of their vision. When the salvage tugs failed to float her at the last high water springs, Harry Fox wagged his head: at the best they might pump her out, at the worst, if the wind changed, she'd be broken on the rocks. The implications of such a disaster are so appalling the summer people no longer discuss the possibility. They are powerless, in any case, to influence the situation: it has become a political issue, an international issue, an ecological issue, a world issue, a moral issue, an inflammatory issue, an historical issue. The salvage tugs hang around like piranhas; television reporters and camera crew have taken over Joe's beach-bar, hoping for the worst. The matter is no longer in the hands of the locals. It never was.

Although she is on their doorstep many of the reports they have received about the tanker's condition have been garbled. No one can understand the delay in starting pumping operations. There is a rumour that she has been holed after all. No one comes ashore from the salvage tugs that lie off and neither the locals sailing close in, nor the television reporters can get any comment from the crews, who fish, sunbathe and wave, but speak a language no one understands. They do not respond to loud-hailers and hams and radio technicians who have tracked down their transmitting and receiving frequency are none the wiser: the exchanges are either in a foreign language, or they are encoded.

Politically, she has become a hot potato. When there was still hope of floating her at the top of springs, no country was willing to receive her. There were intimations, recriminations, accusations even that she had been put on the rocks for the insurance. One power wanted to bomb her. They had the right, Harry Fox explained: under Intervention Protocol any coastal state could act even outside her territorial waters.

At the start, though they were powerless, all the locals had theories about how to save the wreck or what would become of it. Perhaps because they were powerless they felt the need to speculate, to exchange fantasies, to pretend that the destiny of this blot on their landscape was within their control.

Bea recalls another case like this a few years ago, in another country. There were riots on the beach, tear gas used to disperse protesters. 'D'you remember?' she says to Herman. 'It wouldn't happen now, would it. It's odd. People still care but they seem to be paralysed, even the young. Especially the young. A barbecue I should think, wouldn't you? Quite simple: sausages, coleslaw, that sort of thing.'

Herman has dozed off.

Like Worthy he twitches in his sleep, dreaming of falling from imaginary aeroplanes. This time someone left a cargo-loading door unsecured and at the top of their climb everyone, still wearing seat-belts, was sucked out. The descent was quite leisurely and Herman had time to observe the beauty of the earth: snow-capped mountains, blue ocean, shining cities, neat fields patrolled by red farm machines. The pilot, attached to a parachute, passed him going down. Herman could have sworn the bastard winked.

Toby has kissed Mercy. It was a quick grabbed, fantastic sensation, rather salty. They both lie on fossil beach, having swum. They have sand in their hair, salt in their eyes.

Toby looks at the sky. He says: 'You're not going to believe this, but that's the first time I've kissed a girl. Properly. I think I'd rather you didn't tell Tike. I'm an anachronism.'

Mercy squeezes his hand. She says anxiously: 'I'm not a virgin, you know.' He wishes she wouldn't go on but she says: 'It was at the hospital, last time, when I was getting better and they let us out for a few hours a day. To get used to normal living, you know. On parole. There was this boy. We were both lonely, that was all.'

Toby keeps his voice reasonable and understanding. 'D'you still see him?'

'He's dead now.' Mercy draws her finger across her throat.

Toby sits up abruptly on one elbow. 'My God – you mean he cut his throat?'

'It's all right. It's not nearly so bad as people think when you're inside something like that. It has its own rules.'

'But a knife!'

'Sleeping pills aren't very reliable, you know. Unless you get it exactly right you vomit them up. Then they drag you back.'

Toby flops onto the sand again, winded. You kiss a girl and

find yourself in a charnel house. He thinks sometimes that he has led a very sheltered life; at the same moment he is ashamed to feel a leap of excitement: this girl can be his and, like Desdemona, Toby is full of wonder for the horrors she has known. Not just to make love to her but to snatch her back, by love to cure her – what a famous victory that would be!

The sun is hot on his chest. Toby feels strong and hungry. He shifts his position slightly, bends over Mercy and slips down her bikini top.

That evening the family Tyler are eating their supper round the kitchen table. Bea has done a tuna salad and they drink chilled lager. She and Herman are talking, it is a companionable meal. Only Timbo seems rather quiet.

My son, Bea thinks. She frets a little about Timbo: he looks as if he's caught the sun. He's eating too fast and doesn't seem to hear when he's spoken to. Whoever is this lanky stranger sitting at her table in T-shirt and shorts made from faded hacked-off jeans, barefoot, his long hair tangled and bleached (the only row she and Herman have ever had about Timbo's upbringing was over the length of his hair)? Bea thinks: we haven't handled this summer very well. We should have packed him off abroad, sent him to camp at least. Better still, we should have found out what he *wanted* to do. If he knows?

'Timbo? I said the club's having a dinghy race in the bay tomorrow. You could go?'

Bea brings the coffee to the table. At dusk they'll be needing a lamp soon. The summer is more than half over. At this time in the evening the light is drained from the earth. The sky digests and converts all that wonderful colour, and blazes.

Bea lights her cigarette and wonders – she's so fond of Mercy, as a daughter, but not altogether sure how she feels about Timbo spending so much time with her.

'Timbo?'

'I've been meaning to say,' says Timbo. 'I wish you wouldn't call me that.'

8

'BUT WHAT IF we get a thunderstorm?'

'We never have a storm at this time of year.'

Herman grunts dolefully. He and Bea are in bed. They woke early and made morning love; a long time since they've done that. For some reason they both seem to need comfort. Bea reaches for his hand.

'I know what you mean. I thought of ducking the party this year. It's absurd, isn't it. One does what's expected. I don't really mind though. I suppose there may not be many more.'

'Expecting Armageddon?'

'No. I just mean it won't be the same again.'

'Timbo's got to fly the nest sometime.'

'Not just that. I've been thinking. Would you mind if we didn't go back to the city? We'd have to keep a flat, of course. I mean when Timbo's gone.'

Herman does his best to hide his panic. He dislikes change. 'You'd like that?' She nods. 'Then we'll think about it.'

A little later, in the bathroom, he has begun to think of reasons not to change.

'You know what it's like here in winter.'

'Well, we'll see,' says Bea, bathing while he shaves. She soaps her breasts. She's pleased with her neat figure but she feels sad.

They go back to it in bed that night. Now it's come up, it is as though the question (no – the argument) has been with them for a long time and they have chosen to ignore it, like a rat in the wainscot.

Both know they are not really talking about where they should live but about their marriage. About what will happen to their marriage when Timbo goes. About old scores: what Bea was up to that winter in the museum, why Herman went to Madrid when his father was dying. Herman's hypochondria and fear. The centre of Bea's nature which may be cold and monstrous. Timbo's role in this: if all these years it is their son's loving and reconciling genius that has joined their hands and blessed them.

'I don't see why you have to be so stubborn.'

Calmly: 'I don't see why you can't talk about it reasonably.'

'I wish you wouldn't smoke in bed.'

'You really mean that, don't you,' Bea says with forensic interest. 'You actually believe we are going to burst into flames and the house will burn down and we'll all be dead.'

'The insurance on wooden houses is crippling. There must be a reason.'

'Oh my God, Oh my dear God! Herman,' – says Bea carefully, spacing her words as for a child – 'we are all going to die. Our hearts will stop and we will be buried or burned. Scattered. But to think about it as you do – do you ever think about anything but death?' Bea can't stay in bed any more. She gets up and paces the room.

'I think about you. And Timbo.'

She turns on him. 'Yes. You think about us dying! If I have an accident I have to keep it from you. What you'd do if I were ill, I can't imagine. And Timbo – you're always expecting something terrible to happen to him. When he was small you thought he was going to die every time he got a cold. If he went out he'd be kidnapped or run over. Now he can do what he wants you're waiting all the time for him to drown or crash the car. You never really think about him, Timbo, but about his death and how it will affect you. Admit it!'

'I love him.'

'That's *love*?'

'He seems fine.'

'He's like a middle-aged man – hadn't you noticed? Our

124

teenaged son is about forty-five.' Bea has flopped down on the bed again and, astonishingly, she who never cries is crying. 'We go on about how lucky we are, he's no problem, look at the Foxes and the Bonifaces and the Willings – and sometimes I wonder what we've done to him, if he'll ever forgive us.'

'I don't know what you're talking about, Bea. I don't think you're talking about Timbo at all. Or you can't forgive yourself for something. Whatever is is, I'd rather not know about it.'

'That's it exactly, Herman. You never want to know about anything, do you, in case it might hurt? You can't fact the fact that this is a violent world. It's not pretty. Perhaps you're right in a way – we're all killers or victims. Murder's at the centre. Death qualifies everything. It's a wonder we don't all go mad. But I won't, I won't give way like you.'

Bea is standing again now and Herman follows her, hesitates, tries to catch her arm. She pulls away, and then she slaps him hard on the face.

Herman touches his cheek as though he expected to find blood.

'Hush.'

They look at one another, astonished, alarmed to have called up such monsters.

They lie back to back all night. In the morning Bea wakes early, lays a tray carefully, brushes her hair and takes the tray in to Herman in bed.

'I'm staying here,' she says, quite calmly. 'You can do what you like. But if you leave, I'm not coming with you.'

She walks on the beach, barefoot. She looks at the sea and the lighthouse. She bends to pick up a shell: it is rosy and convoluted; it fits her palm exactly.

The walls of the beach-house are thinner than his parents allow for. Toby listened last night – he could hardly help hearing – and was appalled. At first he tried putting his fingers in his ears, then he pulled a pillow over his head but that was suffocating. How many times must Mercy have gone through this, and he couldn't take one night. What had he done to them? He couldn't think. All he wanted to do was to go in and yell at them: stop rowing.

Toby couldn't understand the violence of his reaction. To hear his parents behaving like enemies was as though some previously peace-loving species had suddenly gone mad and turned on its own kind. Which was surely no reason for turning on them?

At last they were quiet, but Toby still couldn't sleep. He thought of Mercy's lover cutting his throat: so much blood. He pulled on his jeans and went down to the beach. The troglodytes were huddled by the breakwaters: a girl looked up and smiled at him. A motorbike on the coast-road ripped the quiet night, then it was still. Toby looked beyond the sleepers, far above the bay and the lighthouse and the wreck, up at the boundless sky, and breathed deeply, as if he could swallow infinity.

'What do you keep going to the window for?'

In the watch-tower on Jeannie's cliff, where no one ever goes, Toby shrugs and grins, lies down beside Mercy and kisses her breasts. He has passed the first astonishment. Simply to lie in her is wonderful, and then to gently move. But he's learning. She likes him to violate her or to pretend to violate her, to plunge into her hard, and then her orgasm is stricken and shuddering. He wonders if he's doing something wrong? Why should it be so painful?

'What's wrong?' Now Mercy wants to comfort him.

'My parents had a fight.'

Mercy looks up at him.

'What was it about?'

'I don't know really. Partly me. It seemed to come from nowhere and yet in a way I wasn't surprised.'

'What did you feel?'

'Responsible.'

Mercy sighs. 'Yes, I know. But you mustn't. It's very

important not to feel that. It doesn't help anyway. You must think about yourself.'

Toby kisses her shoulder without intent. It's nice this, just talking. He teases her: 'Like you do?'

'I am told,' says Mercy sternly, 'that I am reacting neurotically to a bad parental situation. Apparently it is fine to be distressed up to a point and then one must stop. The only thing is, they don't tell you how to stop. You're not supposed to take sides, either. That's absurd, of course, that nearly kills you, trying to be fair. It can't be done.' Mercy shifts and drops her gaze, describes little circles with her finger in the palm of his hand. 'Shall I tell you something terrible? You probably only get better when you feel nothing for either of them any more. Otherwise you just go on hurting yourself.'

'My poor love.'

'Don't worry. I think I'm beginning to learn. I might even decide to live.'

'What did happen? You've never really said.'

Mercy smiles and kisses his eyes. 'You don't want to hear. Drugs, stupid things, some things they know nothing about. I understand if I'd turned and yelled at them, none of this would have happened to me. But I hate violence. Families are violent, aren't they? Except yours. You mustn't take too much notice of one row. Your parents have the only happy marriage I know.'

'Till last night.'

'You really are worried?' she says.

'Not now. Not any more,' says Toby, lying. Because if he does not lie, however will she let him save her? For that has now become his mission: to save Mercy from all ills, to bring her back from the dead. He must be strong. He wishes there were a dragon to kill – or a dinosaur would do.

Toby feels so filled with Mercy, all the ways she opens to him, the incredible discoveries of the flesh he has made in the last week, it does not at first occur to him that he has lost his virginity. When the thought does strike him he grins and thinks of Tike – but will tell no one, least of all Tike. For some reason it appears important to guard the secret he has with Mercy: the ways of the world with love do not seem kindly to him.

Though Bea will guess, he supposes. She may already have guessed. Whether she will be pleased or angry, or indifferent, Toby is not anxious to discover. He takes care to cover his tracks, to spend or appear to spend no more time with Mercy than he ever has. He can't help worrying even that this wonderful event in his life might have left some mark upon him: he looks in the mirror and sees nothing different.

There is one moment of alarm, when Bea looks up from her sewing and says: 'It's not too late for you to join Tike at camp. If you want to go?'

'No thanks. I'd rather stay here.'

Bea snaps off the thread and reaches for more. Working by the porch light in the dusk, Bea wears a thin shawl and wire-framed spectacles (my mother being a Good Woman again, thinks Toby).

'It can't be very exciting for you here. You need people your own age'. (She knows about Mercy and wants to break us up?)

'It's fine. And those camps aren't so marvellous, you know. Like joining the army.'

'You haven't quarrelled with Tike?'

'Not exactly. Well, I suppose we've grown apart a little. Temporarily. Anyhow, I truly do like it here.'

Bea looks over her spectacles, touches his hand. 'Well, it's lovely for us to have you.' She peers into the darkness. 'Can you see my thimble?'

'Here.' Toby picks up the thimble from where it has rolled in a crack between the boards, gives it to his mother, then he kisses her cheek lightly. 'I think I'll go for a walk.'

Bea opens her mouth to say 'Careful', and then checks herself, wondering whatever harm she imagines might lie in wait for her son, walking on the beach. She's never been that kind of mother – fretting after him. She's behaving like Herman and must cure herself.

As a sensible woman, Bea makes an effort to concentrate on her sewing, but her mind wanders. She sits with her hands in her lap. 'Well, cat,' she says, 'what is becoming of us?' She feels desolate. Moths cluster around the porch lamp. A shot rings out.

Sitting with Mercy in the Willings's abandoned boat-house, Toby says: 'I'm really not sure she's noticed anything. She's very preoccupied at the moment.'

'They're still rowing?'

'Not exactly. But there's a fight going on underneath. She tried to send me away today. What about yours?'

In the darkness Mercy says: 'He hit her again, but sometimes I think she asks for it. No – I mean she *wants* it.'

Their knees are touching. Toby seizes her wrists. 'Why don't we go away? Mercy – let's go.'

'I'm a policeman,' she says. 'I can't let them kill one another.'

They make love. It's kinky somehow in the darkness; fantastic recognising all the parts of her by touch, lips, tongue, groin. He's learned to hold back, hold off, taste, retreat, advance. Mercy puts her hand to his chest. 'What's that noise?'

'A car back-firing. The motorbikes.'

'No.'

'I love you', Toby says wildly: he feels as though he had actually entered her bloodstream. He swims upwards.

'No!' she says, her face turned away, stricken. 'It was a gun.'

Erin on the telephone: 'Did you hear that, Bea? They're shooting people now! Bea, are you there? I can't find Mercy! Where's Timbo?'

Francine's husky vodka voice, several seas over: 'Oh, Bea – you don't think Merlyn's shot Erin? Harry's out. Is Herman out? If Merlyn's shot Erin I couldn't forgive myself. Bea – could Harry have shot Merlyn?'

Bea gropes for her cigarettes. 'Erin's all right, Francine, I just spoke to her. I'm going to hang up now, then I'll ring the police.'

'What's happened?' cries Herman. 'O, my God, where's Timbo?'

'I can't get through to emergency. Where's the police number?'

'It's not listed. Where's my gun?' Herman's trying to behave well but he's frantic – all his worst dreams coming home to roost.

'Not listed?' Bea repeats dully. She sits down by the telephone and hugs her shawl around her, as though she were cold. This is an emergency, yet she feels overwhelmed by a need to curl up and sleep. She rubs her eyes and looks up at her husband. 'What gun?'

'My gun.'

'I didn't know you had a gun?'

False alarm. No emergency. In the dusk Jeannie Fisk has carried out her threat and conducted a single-handed dog hunt. There are always one or two stragglers after the pack has left at sunset. Firing from her beach-buggy, Jeannie winged one but it got away and died somewhere else. So, in a sense, nothing happened.

There is, of course, an inquest.

'But Jeannie,' says Herman reasonably. 'You simply cannot go around shooting dogs.'

'They're a health hazard,' says Jeannie.

Francine agrees: 'They raid the dustbins every night.'

'Poor doggies,' says Erin. Later she confides to Bea: 'I believe that Jeannie is a very violent woman.'

'Aren't we all,' says Bea.

The day of the Tylers' party is the hottest yet. The air shakes and by noon the lighthouse is a trembling mirage, suspended between sea and sky; the wreck has become, for the moment, a figment – its shark's-fin shape all but dissolved. No sail can stir. The outboard putters across the bay carrying the picnic to the lighthouse island. So uncertain is the configuration of the island, they seem to be moving towards a fantasy or a dream, they will always be making the passage, they will never arrive; they will arrive and it will all be melted, their wonderful vision, into thin air.

But after all the dory bites on the shingle and the engine coughs out. Toby raises the propeller and Mercy and Bea step ashore, carrying the basket between them. The warm sea licks the hem of their jeans and Mercy wears the most romantic straw hat: a wonderful, nostalgic, latticed concoction, the colour of violets under deep greenery, tied beneath the chin by a scarf, an exhausted pink. Her face is dappled, her hair cloudy, her nails are bitten, her breasts small, her feet scuffed, her shoulders like folded wings, yet somehow this pre- posterous hat redeems her – Mercy is hestitating on the edge of beauty, thinks Bea.

They stow the makings of the party in the dark, circular room beneath the lighthouse. In war this had been converted to a gun-emplacement, a ready-made pillbox, with corrugated iron shutters over the gun ports. Later, the lighthouse keepers used it for storage but since automation no one comes here except for a few lovers – it is a dank and dreary place neglected even by the trippers who land on the island a few times in summer. Or maybe they never discover it: sharp, prickly sea-grass and thorn keeps the entrance secret.

It is good though, for the Tylers' purpose – cool and private.

Bea paddles in the white sand, looking as ever for shells, fossils, history. It was extraordinary what the earth would yield, if you knew what you were looking for. Such tales it could tell, both of violence and survival – the death of the harmless Ammonites, for instance: as sudden and mysterious as Tyrannosaurus's extinction. Whole species wiped out because they found themselves ill-equipped to survive in an altered world. And those who did survive, altered.

At the same time Bea drew some inexplicable solace from

these dead companions; the marks, the traces, the carapaces, the prints they left, appeared as messages, signals across the millenia as bright as the cold glow of extinguished stars.

Not given to fancy, preferring as a rule dryness, nevertheless Bea would stand – as she does now – on the edge of the ocean, like a man looking up at a clear night sky, and feel the tug or the nudge of the tide at her feet; and appreciate at some level both instinctive and intellectual that she was a part – for one short moment aware and sentient – of a vast and complex process whose end was as uncertain as its beginning.

Sometimes, though faithless, she does not fear death at all. Back into the evolutionary soup.

Jeannie said once: 'What's the point? All that fuss to get us here then someone pulls the plug. This place is on the way out. Even plumbers don't make house-calls any more.'

'Assuming we're the centre of the universe.'

'If we're not, then why don't cows talk?'

Bea decided to let it go. 'Because if they talked they might have to give parties.'

Jeannie snorted. 'You and Darwin.'

'Yes, I'd like to go to the Galapagos.'

'When I was young,' says Toby, 'for years I thought my mother had lost something, when we went for walks. Then she said she was looking for shells.'

Mercy asks him: 'Do you remember when we buried that tern?'

'I'd forgotten. I'd rather forget. That whole business was idiotic. I killed that bird really.'

'It would have died anyway.'

They have rounded the lighthouse and there is a darkness: the wreck ledged on the rocks, her bows biting into the sandy bar.

Mercy is crouched over a rock pool. As she disturbs it with her finger an albino crab scuttles for shelter and the water clouds.

'Are you frightened of death?' she says, settling back and waiting for the pool to clear.

Bea's out of sight, scavenging on the sea-shore. Toby too hunches down and runs his finger along the tender inside of Mercy's wrist.

'Not today.'

Mercy frowns. 'Be serious.' The light so dazzles him he cannot read her face beneath the wonderful hat.

'All right. Mostly I don't think about it for months on end, then I'm frightened out of my wits. I used to think it was a dinosaur my mother took me to see in a museum one winter. I had nightmares about that for years. I got confused, you see: the dinosaur wasn't the killer, he was just another victim. Then my grandfather died and I had to be with him, because my father was away and my mother was with my grand-mother. That was quite a winter. I liked him. They kept saying he was so old, he'd have got iller, but I kept thinking death didn't make any sense; I knew he didn't want to die, *he* didn't think he was old enough to die – no one ever is.' Then Toby remembers this is no way for Orpheus to talk to Eurydice. 'No,' he says firmly, 'I'm not scared of death.'

Bea is calling from down the beach.

With the dory empty now, they decide to row back. Toby takes the oars, Bea rides at the bow and Mercy in the stern, facing Toby, trails her seaweed hand in the water, her thin wrist wavy and attenuated, her bones of coral made; and she dips her head in the wonderful hat beneath which the sea changes her face too, so that it becomes liquid, less frangible. She is all violets and sea-shades, thinks Bea: of course he loves her.

Harry Fox knows about barbecues. He knows about com-puters, the entrails of cars, the mysteries of plumbing and electrical wiring, porch-building and barbecues. From the same instinct perhaps, to make sense of the material world, he actually enjoys cooking: good cooking being an orderly process, a gesture, in a small way, against chaos (Bea knows this too: most women do).

So it is Harry (rather than hapless Herman) who ferries the

Portable-Patio-Bar-B-Q out to the lighthouse island and sets it up; and it is Harry who will tend the charcoal and cook tonight. And for a while, as he sizzles sausages and spare ribs, Harry can forget decision-making computers, and Francine, and Francine and lobsters, and whatever Francine is up to, if anything, with Merlyn Willings – and Harry can believe for a while in a universe that is not altogether mad. A world of virtue, of friends good and true? Hardly. But at least there are still simple tasks to be done. Harry regards himself as a simple man and he is often in pain for a world that seems to mutilate itself against the cutting edge of its self-made troubles. Bea, he thinks, understands this, but her stance is detached, drier. Harry toils up the beach, assembles the barbecue and goes for a paddle. Optimism returns. It will be a fine night.

Herman is not sure what is going on between himself and Bea. A temporary truce appears to have been called while the preparations for the party go on but it seems to him to be a fragile peace. Watching her return from shopping, work in the kitchen, shred salad, pack it in plastic boxes, mix the dressing and pour it in litre bottles to transport, frown slightly over her lists, tick off another item, Herman thinks how extraordinary, how competent and ordered his wife is, what a wonder. Everyone says. Then the night of the row this ordered, competent, peaceful woman he loved had torn at her own breast like a pelican. Revealing something frantic, disorder, the wildest chaos.

At one point he had seized her by the shoulders and yelled in her face: 'I love you!'

'Oh, love,' she had said flatly. 'What does it have to do with love.'

It was not her age: her hormones were still in fine order. Nor Timbo going away – or not entirely.

It seems as though their happy marriage has concealed many secrets and evasions, and now these oubliettes have been opened, God knows what staring skeletons may be revealed. Herman shivers. Dusk falls. Time to go to the party. Herman doesn't like parties but this one, he knows, means a lot to Bea; she wants it to be like the old times and if anyone can bring it off, Bea can. And if she can, perhaps all will be as it was before. Or have they invented the past? Is that too one of the ploys of evasion? Herman opens a cupboard, a drawer, and wonders where his gun did go. He sits down in his study, the large, sandy man, man of sand, and rubs his eyes. Someone's calling: we must go, we must go to the island. He pours himself a whisky and swallows it in a gulp, then he remembers – he threw it away. Bought it against terrorists, hijackers, burglars, rabid dogs, then knew quite well he could never bring himself to use it and chucked it away. Guns cause accidents. Never never let your gun pointed be at anyone. As the spirits hit his stomach something strikes Herman as funny. He has another drink, strides out of his house locking the cat in and the burglars out, walks down the beach, steps into the dory and someone calls: come on, we must go to the island.

9

'OH, BEA' – ERIN squats on the sand, hugging her knees –
'this is so lovely, a lovely party. But where's Timbo?'

'He and Mercy are swimming out.'

Erin shudders. 'How brave.'

'The sea's warm. And Mercy's much stronger.'

Erin turns to Bea a rapturous face: 'Yes, she is, isn't she? I
knew if she stayed she'd be all right. I *knew* this was the
summer Mercy would get better! And Timbo's so sweet with
her.'

'Yes, he's very fond of her. We all are.'

'D'you think they're lovers?' Erin looks wistful.

'I should think they probably are.'

Word has got round about the swim and everyone waits for
the lovers to rise from the sea. No one would use the word
magic, but it is as if the party attends a blessing. Meanwhile,
drink and the balmy night eases some, excites others; there is
a crackle in the air: maybe Herman is right about the
thunderstorm.

Harry sweats happily over his barbecue. Those who have had
to go to the city recently exchange congratulatory horror
stories about how bad it is there – garbage in the streets,
muggings, fires, services breaking down; at night most shops
sport riot shutters against vandalism; there are more terrorists
than tourists and the only tourists who come any more are the
Japanese to photograph the dumps of uncollected refuse in

the main squares. Harry has run a programme through the computer and come up with a projection of the complete collapse of law and order in the city.

'When does it get here?' says Jeannie, downing her white wine from a paper cup (she splices the wine with spirits from a flask she keeps in her beach-bag).

Bea shrugs. The two women are sitting on a rug. Jeannie buries the stub of her menthol cigarette in the sand, and immediately lights another.

'What's the trouble with you and Herman?'

'What trouble?'

'You've had a fight.'

'Everyone has fights.'

'Not you and Herman. You're the ones who lived happily ever after – an example to us all.'

Bea stretches. People are swimming. The water is very soft tonight.

'Jeannie, I don't know. Who knows about these things? Perhaps no ideal marriage is what it seems. Don't you think?'

'I don't know,' says Jeannie. 'I haven't seen many of them. Yours was the only one.'

'Bless you, Jeannie. I'd better go and help Harry.'

'It's a great party.'

After an uncertain start, it is indeed a good party. Faces and anxieties are blurred. They move around the beach, drinking, smiling, touching, and are sometimes struck speechless by the low sky sagging with stars; the air is furry and electric at once, and every so often there is a flash of green on the horizon. They gulp the air like a thick dark drink. They are tranced. The barbecue is their hearth and every so often they return to it like children to be fed, then drift away again or stroll in the cool sand. On this side of the island, facing the mainland, they are hardly aware of the looming wreck behind them – to see it they would have to skirt the beach or climb to the lighthouse.

They splash in the phosphorescent water, race out to

Jeannie's Chris Craft. Francine, who seems happy tonight and less stoned than usual, dives deep to swim under the motor-boat and comes up spluttering and laughing, waving her bikini top. Harry, freed from his barbecue duties by Tonio Boniface, gives chase, churning the water like a cheerful dog, kisses her breasts while Merlyn floats aloof on his back pursued by the pregnant pink balloon of Betty Boniface: she'll never catch him. Herman swims, as he always does, carefully, and Bea, for this moment on this night, in this kind sea, is content to keep pace with him and sedately they swim to the shore.

The air is thickening. On the mainland it would be very close.

They flop on the beach. The cool sand prickles their skins and there is something about the quality of the air or of the barely breathing darkness that makes them speak softly. Bea and Herman and Francine and Harry and Erin and Merlyn, murmur and sigh and smile, and play do-you-remember.

Do you remember when.

'D'you remember when Timbo cut his foot on a razor-shell?'

D'you remember other picnics, other parties, other summers, all those summers so sweetly scented packed away? When accidents were small?

(The girl from the fishing shack runs along the beach her hair flaming like Medusa from a furnace, but we won't remember that. Not tonight.)

'Do you remember Jeannie's writers?'

'Oh God. *That* summer.'

The friends smile at each other, proud. Of what? Of having survived perhaps. And more or less kept their looks: oh, the sagging belly here and there is Merlyn's iron hair flecked with grey and they are older – but it's wonderful what friendship can do to keep time at bay. The grey becomes Merlyn as lichen upon stone; Bea was never pretty but this is the prime of her handsomeness.

It's their friendship though of which they are proud. As if they were eternally connected – limbs entwined, cheek pressed to cheek, at moments like this of deepest unspoken

138

and often unforeseen intimacy, a sense almost of sharing the same bloodstream, tissue, heart; as if one were hurt the others would cry out.

The sand trickles between Francine's bare breasts, Erin rests against Merlyn's shoulder and he lets her. Harry lies flat on his back counting the stars, his head in Francine's lap while Bea at one end and Herman at the other exchange wordlessly the flick of a question: well, what about us, what do we do now?

Bea picks up a handful of the cold white sand and lets it run through her fingers. It's like snow. There come into her mind, unsummoned, intimations of winter. It's a slight breeze that has come up from nowhere, ruffled the water and died away, leaving behind the memory of a chill as though a door had been opened and quickly shut. Bea shivers and Erin looks at her.

'Goose on my grave.'

The moment of closeness has gone, it was evanescent, very fragile, the breeze dissolved it, it is dissolved.

Merlyn, with Erin still resting against him, leans over Francine and dangles a bunch of grapes between her breasts and Bea sees in Harry's face a look of such pain she wants to take him in her arms. Tonio starts a game of mildly drunken French cricket with a piece of driftwood and a beach ball. Tonio's out and Herman takes his place braving it out, assailed from all sides. Misjudging in the dusk, he bends too low over the bat and the ball strikes his face, bringing tears to his eyes. 'Stop!' Erin cries, 'stop – Herman's hurt!' but he squeezes his eyes shut for a moment, shakes his big head and straightens up and he remembers the violent ball games Jeannie's intellectuals played that summer years ago – a well-known shark-fishing playwright with a bleeding nose, clutching his nose and hopping on one foot like a child with rage and pain as his own blood ran down between his balled fists. And for some reason he cannot connect he has a remembered vision of Bea chopping meat, separating tendon from fat from flesh and the blood on her fingers and Bea, thinking herself unobserved, licking her finger. And the thought had come into Herman's head: Bea is a violent woman.

That would have been the winter after her miscarriage, the winter she said she went to classes and Timbo was ill. (But Bea is practically a vegetarian?) She did eat meat that winter, he recalls: perhaps she was anaemic after the miscarriage.

Wap! His legs sting. Herman's out.

Bea has gone to fetch more wine from the cellar beneath the lighthouse. Walking back, the air seems to creak: it's the wreck, shifting as the tide comes in. Timbo and Mercy will be swimming against the tide. Bea makes her way back through a chain of warm pools just below high-water mark. The air sweats, it presses against her mouth and her eyes. In Harbinger's room that winter they swam sweatily together like amphibians struggling to surface from the porridge of creation. They ate slippery foods: pasta, Greek honey-cake, anything oily, anything sweet. She brought oil to their love-making, they did wild things and then he wrapped himself in the Indian blanket and told her how, according to Harbinger, the world had been made, and she listened like a child to fairy stories. From the making of the world he moved effortlessly to the making of Harbinger and for a time that too enchanted Bea. Her own upbringing, though not repressed, had been so ordinary, so orderly, she was the kind of child who had never needed to be told to tidy her room, she liked order, seemed to need it; and then she married young straight from her tidy room. (Perhaps she had married Herman to tidy him up? Even then he was accident-prone: the first time she met him, at a party, he'd trapped his fingers in his car door and the first six months of their courtship they'd waited for his blackened thumb-nail to fall off.)

Whereas Harbinger – there seemed to be nothing he hadn't tried, seen, tasted, made love to, no trip he hadn't been on (that was the tail-end of the drug era). Bea wondered however he'd managed to get three perfectly good degrees, publish two papers and establish himself as the rising expert on reptiles in the northern hemisphere. His life sounded such chaos.

'Well, you see,' he said, grinning foxily from his cross-legged position on the floor, 'I was an orphan. I believe in freedom.'

'I don't see the connection?'

'Leaving your blood parents is an emotional decision, someone always gets hurt. Walking out on adoptive parents can be quite rational. They never owned you in the first place.'

Then he read her his thesis.

'I don't think that I'm very stable at the moment,' said Bea.

Harbinger dipped his finger in the pot and anointed her nipples with honey. She tipped his penis with honey.

'Yum.'

He slid in. When he came he yelled – a kind of war whoop. It was sticky and hilarious and crazy. He panted like a beached fish trying to grow lungs. 'Why do you wear your hair so short?'

The next time, he said: 'I want you to come and live with me.'

'I can't do that, Paul.'

She couldn't explain. She took a deep breath and walked out into the snow. The point is, Bea felt at that time that she was a little mad and therefore no decision she made could be a good one. Sometimes she has imagined that he moved inside her still, though it would only be a menstrual cramp and Harbinger is dead. Isn't he?

As Bea rounds the corner from the seaward beach the wind whips up and there is a crack of thunder, closer this time, but still no easing rain. In the windy moonlight Bea can see the picnic dancing: cloths flying, rugs lifting and falling, sparks rising from the barbecue; the people too seem to dance, chasing the windborne debris, pulling on shawls and sweaters, swooping on stones to pin down anything that might fly. And

Erin standing on the shore, under the moon, a mad gipsy, her hair torn from its pins, her dun-coloured shift billowing in full sail; while Jeannie's motor boat heaves in the sea, falling and rising, rising and falling – the chain groans, the boat shudders, lifts her white bows and crashes against the incoming wind and sea and lifts her white bows. Where are they? cries Erin, where are the children? And her voice is torn from her throat and whipped away.

Then Timbo and Mercy surface, they are beached, and they stumble up the sand shaking off the bright water, panting with triumph after their long and difficult swim.

At the height of the wind, between the claps, there is a dull sound, not so much an explosion as an implosion, something broken. Harry says the wreck may have been holed on the rocks. No time for that now. The party's over, they must go. The wind falls abruptly light and the air is turned to water as the rain drives down extinguishing the barbecue. The storm is directly overhead, there is hardly a pause between lightning and thunder. They run for the boats. Harry scatters the coals on the beach.

The next morning, walking on the foreshore in the lovely washed daybreak that follows the storm, Toby comes across something dark and oily struggling on the shingle. A cormorant, one of the shyest of birds, grounded. As Toby crouches it pauses in its pathetic suicidal grooming and flaps a heavy wing. Toby looks up. It's just past low water and everywhere the tide has retreated it has left behind black pools. He is not sure what to do with the cormorant. He touches its breast and feels the heart racing. It waves its eel-like neck.

Such a day! Such a day (provided one overlooks the birds and the pools) for a painter, for Erin. The sky has not been so soft since spring, colours everywhere have been dashed in and left to run. But Erin, like most of them, sleeps heavily after the spoiled picnic, groans as she turns over in her sleep while Bea, waking, is dazed by the stare of the slatted blinds; she would like to turn over and sleep again but she slips out of bed, adjusts the blinds for Herman, not to wake him, goes downstairs and plugs in the coffee. She sits at the pine table and waits for the coffee to percolate. Through the flap in the door comes the cat, soaked from last night's storm and furious; its plastered fur elongates and narrows it to something like a primitive cave-drawing of a cat or one of Merry Willings's stick animals – all skull, spine and malice. It won't let Bea dry it but grooms itself, biting at its own fur. Bea sighs, pours herself a black coffee and watches the sun finger the corner of the kitchen table, then spread, illuminating the grainy surface, touching other objects of copper and china and wood, rising up the walls, sparking windows and every shiny thing until it swallows the whole kitchen, floods the whole kitchen with gold.

About the same time Harry Fox runs across the beach in swimming-trunks, breathing in-out-in-hold-it – out-in, and bounds into the sea. And out again, for as far as the eye can see there is a skin of oil on the water, and Toby captures the helpless cormorant in his shirt and carries it home to his mother.

10

THE FIRST HALF dozen Bea washes in detergent, dries, puts in the hospital cage and feeds, with Mercy's and Timbo's help.

'They'll probably die though, they've swallowed so much oil.' It's a disaster beyond her competence, there are too many, every tide washes up more. Bird Rescue takes them off to the sanctuary but even they won't save many.

As a disaster, some spokesman says, it's a drop in the ocean: a remote and unfrequented spot, no fishing industry, few trippers. Yes, perhaps a boom should have been laid across the harbour entrance, but that is a job for the local authority. Anyway, this has been freak weather for the time of year: there was no reason to expect that the wreck would be holed. The enquiry into the wreck continues, blame is exchanged, a conclusion is awaited, evidence taken, a verdict will follow.

Jeannie hoots and points at the headline: WORLD'S OIL SUPPLY RUNS OUT.

When the dispersant crews and the television crews have gone Jeannie shades her eyes and says: 'What the hell is Harry Fox doing?'

Bea, flopped in the porch swing-seat, is tired, washing the birds has tired her out. 'Moving the beach. He's shovelling off the top layer, you see. He's even got the beach-bums at it.'

'Jesus Christ.'

'Fossil beach is all right. We can still swim there. Or your pool. I think you'll find your pool will be popular for the rest of the season.'

'All welcome. Be my guest.'

A terrible day for birds, it has been; a bad day too for fishermen, ornithologists and for the summer people. Yet it is a challenge too – the catastrophe draws them together and for a while Harry is never short of volunteers for his beach-moving exercise.

Even the beach-bums, the sleepers. At first they merely watch, smiling their dreamy smiles, then one unknots his legs, moves in and picks up a shovel. The rest follow. They won't go into the house but when Bea takes down a jug of fresh lemonade they accept and offer her smiles of astonishing radiance. Bea wonders how she could ever have feared them. She begins to look at them individually. Two girls have babies they suckle in the open; when the children cry they rock them in their arms and give them rags to suck – Bea shudders, yet the infants seem healthy enough. They feed each other's babies, she notices, and the boys take equal responsibility. 'Those hippies' says Jeannie, scornfully, but as Bea says, she is out of date. All that is ancient history – the beats, the flower people, the hippies, the punks, gone, all gone into oblivion; and now just these sad, dreamy children sitting out their lives on the beach. Once she thought of asking them what they wanted, and she knows what they would have answered. Nothing.

(Then, of course, there are the motorcyclists on the coast-road every evening. They are a phenomenon of unreason and lately have grown wilder. They wear strange devices on their jackets. No one in his senses challenges them. They rule the night.)

One day they wake to find that the salvage boats have gone. They wonder why. The wreck is still there, lower in the water since her holing on the rocks. The bulk of the oil was spilled the night of the storm, but she is still seeping: every tide is black. Harry's heroic beach-clearing begins to seem a little mad but he will not abandon it. His bald pate and freckled shoulders peel and even when his helpers fall away he continues to shovel from dawn till dusk and cart away and shovel. A brave, touching figure, but if he goes on like this, he'll make himself ill. And he has as much hope of reversing the disaster single-handed as of turning back the tide.

Toby and Mercy go to fossil beach now to swim or to make love – the cave's a good place when the troglodytes are away. They lie together sometimes for hours just tasting and touching and whispering, at ease among the cave-dwellers' debris of rags and bottles and rusting cans. Whatever the weather, the cave always smells cold. It smells as a grave might smell to the newly dead and Mercy, scratching in the sand, finds bones.

Something about his mother and the birds has disturbed Toby. He feels foolish.

'You see, I always thought she could cure anything. She seems to have given up on the birds.'

'And that worries you?'

'No. Yes, I suppose it does. Well, I expect that's normal – to imagine your parents to be infallible.'

'I never did, Not for ages, anyway.'

'Well, none of them are, of course. But it comes as a shock – when you first realise. I must be a late developer.'

Calmly, Mercy says: 'I like the way you're developing.'

But Toby doesn't feel like making love at this moment, he is thinking. 'The museum my mother took me to one winter, or maybe it was the zoo – and I was ill afterwards. I caught a chill, something like that.' Stricken, he sits up to make his anouncement. 'You know, it's only just struck me, for the first time ever, that my mother was up to something! Everything fits: those classes she was supposed to be going to, she always came back different.' The effort of remembering makes Toby squeeze his eyes shut and then he opens them as though presented with a vision, a complete re-run. 'She was a bit mad – wild. I was in bed. It was snowing. I had a temperature. She smelled of incense.'

'Incense?'

'No. No, of course, it must have been joss-sticks. Then one

day I heard her crying and she didn't go to the museum any more.'

Toby flops back. He feels as though he's run a race. He is felled by the discovery that his mother was once a wicked woman.

Mercy laughs at him. 'What do you mean by that? Wicked?'

'Not virtuous. No. What I mean is she was lying, not in words, she wasn't what she seemed. Or what I thought she was. Not necessarily the same thing.'

'What you wanted her to be – isn't that what you mean?'

Toby turns to look at her. 'How d'you know all this?'

Mercy grins. 'My therapist told me.'

'What therapist?'

When Mercy is on the defensive she no longer hides behind that wing of hair but looks out bravely. With Toby at least.

'In hospital. And since. They like you to keep it up. They call it therapy now instead of analysis, not to frighten you, but it comes to the same thing. Anyhow. I didn't learn very much but I did learn that: parents and children have ideas of each other. They rarely correspond. We all want motherly mothers.'

Toby laughs. 'All summer I've been bracing myself to walk out on her and now I find she walked out on me years ago. Or that's how it feels.'

'You're over-reacting. Bea needs you more than she ever did.'

'She's ruthless.'

'Bea's human. That's all.'

'Why do we spend so much time talking about them?'

Mercy shakes her head. She doesn't know everything. By any means.

In the late afternoon a pencil of sun enters the cave. Mercy has found these bones. The troglodytes are vegetarian, so it can't be them. Bea would know.

147

Five of the birds died, one lives. It's a rapacious, clumsy creature with a sideways gait and an appetite that will not be filled. It becomes very tame and whenever anyone comes near hops around the cage demanding attention; it will even take food from the hand and watches everything that goes on with a sharp experienced eye. For some reason the gangster cat is alarmed by it, while Herman, who has never shown much interest in Bea's invalids, visits the bird several times a day, like an anxious relative at a bedside. He discovers it likes grapes and feeds them through the mesh. He seems to have a vested interest in its survival. They make an odd couple: the big fair man crouched on his haunches and the black sea-bird. When Bea approaches them they look up at her, four eyes. She feels excluded.

Bea has a feeling of desolation, of her occupation gone. This will pass, she knows, it's like influenza or a touch of madness. Am I a little mad, she wonders? And breaks one of her favourite dishes, a white bowl with blue flowers, cuts herself collecting the shards and thinks did she break the favourite dish because she cannot mend the birds – any more than she can see how, at this moment, she might mend her marriage. She may even have wilfully broken her marriage just as surely as she might have flung the dish to the floor. There is a source of dark unreason in her that pumps rage into her blood.

Timbo and Mercy are telling her about bones, some bones they have found. They are standing on the porch, with the sun behind them, talking about bones. Bea had been sitting in the rocking chair, her hands in her lap, folded in on herself, and then across her lap falls their shadow. Beyond them, Herman is sitting in a deckchair on the scorched lawn, wearing a white sun-hat, talking to the bird. The bird cocks its head and watches him with bright sceptical eyes.

*

148

Bea does not move, except to lock her fingers together in her lap as though to save herself from flying apart – she imagines scraps and flakes of herself, like sparks from a fire, whirling into the white mid-afternoon air to form a dust daemon, to fall as ash. For it strikes her suddenly – as one of those illuminations that work in the soul for months and years – that she never cared for her mother because they were alike. And who can bear for long a speaking mirror?

'What bones?'
  'In the cave.'
  'I covered them up again,' says Mercy.

What are they talking about, thinks Bea, bones and caves? She remembers Sarah, her mother, it feels almost as though she had called her up from the grave or the air or the cutting light. And there was Sarah – so vital everyone said, so brave. Your mother is remarkable – how many times had Bea heard that? Sarah kept life on a short rein and told it what to do; even at the end would not acknowledge that it had got out of hand, bolted. But this vitality for which Sarah had been famous – Bea sees now, it was anger. Both she and Sarah had been born in a rage at the disorder of life. And if life was an untidy sister with whom one had to share a room, death was the greatest disorder of all.

Not just a matter of tidiness, of course, but of will. A deep, secret dread of anything that challenged the embattled will: accident, weather, illness, grief. And fear made monsters of them both – Sarah the bully, Bea the comforter, there was hardly a pin between them.

Bea calls out to her husband on the lawn: we're going to the caves.

She is tired, she hardly has the strength to walk as far as fossil beach. How odd, Bea thinks: Herman and Timbo and myself, all only ones. A larger family, between themselves, might somehow have managed to dilute Sarah, I might have liked her better, given brothers and sisters. Is that what Timbo feels?

Herman is excited because the bird has managed today, for the first time, to flap its wings. If Herman could fly, he wouldn't have to go in aeroplanes, then he would not crash, or be sucked out of a depressurised cabin or be eaten in the Andes or have to eat some fellow-passenger. He looks up at his wife, walking away from him along the beach, and sees Bea as punishing herself for something he cannot understand, walking away – and her figure shakes in the sun, she is shattered by light, the light devours her.

By the time they reach fossil beach, Bea feels dizzy, she understands she must carry her head very carefully, like a bowl of water that might spill. The cave smells invitingly cold yet she is reluctant to go in. Mercy says: here, you see, I covered them with sand. She is talking about bones. Paul Harbinger kept his own private collection of reptile skulls and once when they'd smoked pot Bea heard them scream and saw them grin. When Sarah was dying her hair came out in little tufts: you could see the scalp. Bea, combing the poor dead hair from the brush, caught Sarah watching her, her mouth turned down.

Standing in the cave (with Sarah? Sarah seems very close), Bea suddenly agrees with her mother: yes, death *is* an insult. At any age, a termination as unacceptable as a traffic accident. The cave smells of death, it has the scent of the charnel house and Bea, brushing the sand from the bones, sees the grave-marks on the back of her hands. It's not the world, it's our age that makes us dinosaurs.

It's so simple, she smiles.

The world is not coming to an end. We are.

They crouch around the bones, Bea kneeling. Two of the

troglodytes have returned to the cave and join them. The bones are quite small.

'Animal?' says Mercy. 'They must be mammal?'

Bea is shaky on mammals, but there is no doubt about this.

'Human,' she says. 'Look how the bones are arranged – it must be a grave. A child. A girl, I think. See where the skull seems to have been fractured.'

They are all awed. One of the cave-dwellers, the boy, reaches out and touches the cheekbone, very gently.

How recent, thinks Bea? Who to call – a policeman or an archaeologist? It was a violent death, that's certain. Suddenly she is saddened by these bones, her dryness deserts her, she feels like a violator, a breaker of tombs. Let her rest. Carefully, with the feeling of performing a necessary ritual, she covers the tiny pelvis that cradled nothing, pours sand into the bone circlets of blind eyes.

'Nothing, just a headache. I felt dizzy in the sun.'

The habit of not alarming Herman is so strong in her, Bea said to Timbo: don't tell your father, it's just the heat, I'll be down for supper. And now there is Herman, standing in the doorway, large and worried. I am not going to die, she thinks of saying – though perhaps I have seen death? Is that how Herman sees it? Herman is the most terrible hoverer around sickrooms – anxious for the victim, yet fearing contagion.

'Oh, Herman, for heaven's sake, either come in or go out.'

'If you'll be all right?'

'I'm fine. I'll be fine.'

When Herman has gone Bea lies, her cheek against the pillow. Stillness. She feels if she can stay still, take shallow breaths, she may ride this flood of unreason. Yet this stillness is as exhausting as running.

In her dream she is scratching with her nails in sand to uncover her own grave. Don't they know? They have buried me alive, says Sarah who is also Bea, and there, crucified above an ant-hill, is Harbinger eaten by ants. They go for the soft parts first, the eyes and the sex.

When Bea wakes, sweating, it is evening, supper-time, she can hear the house talking of supper, the fridge door opening and closing, the clatter of a dish, the radio snapping on, off, the slap of feet on the stairs then a whisper, retreat, the water pipes grumbling, talk below she cannot make out as though she had forgotten the language. She feels as she used to waking in some foreign town where she knew no one, after a long journey. One arrived in the middle of the night, slept ravenously and woke without bearings to the cry of women and children and birds in a centre courtyard visitors never entered; there was always a radio, women doing laundry, a bright bird in a cage singing, singing.

Bea gets up, showers, takes an aspirin, slips on a thin blue cotton robe and towelling mules, pulls the brush through her hair and goes downstairs. Herman and Toby look up from their plates. They look alarmed at the sight of her. Herman at once pushes away his plate, wipes his mouth and half-stands. Toby is watching them both.

Herman says: 'You needn't get up. There's no need to get up. We could bring you something to eat.'

'No, I don't want anything to eat.'

'Why don't you go back to bed?'

They looked quite cheerful when she first came into the kitchen. She had the feeling she had interrupted something. She has a weird feeling of looking in at her own life through a window. Timbo looks down at his plate and pushes the food around rather than eats it.

'No,' says Bea. 'I think I'll get dressed. I'll go for a drive.'

Herman follows her up the stairs and into the bedroom. He follows her to the clothes-cupboard. Bea can hear Timbo listening below.

'If you want to go out I'll drive you.'

'If you don't mind, I want to go by myself.'

She is halfway through dressing, Herman reaches out as though to grab her by the shoulders, then in a movement like a sigh he lets his arms fall to his sides and sits on the edge of the bed, his big head bowed.

Bea looks in the mirror to check her shirt fastening and

would like to smash the mirror in which she sees the man sitting on the edge of the bed and the crazy woman and the marriage between them, stronger perhaps than both of them.

'I don't like you driving around alone,' says Herman. And then: 'If we're quarrelling I'd like to know what we're quarrelling about.'

'I just have a headache, that's all,' says Bea. She kisses Herman lightly on the top of his head, picks up the car keys from the dressing-table and runs downstairs and out to the car. Timbo is feeding the waste-disposal unit. He doesn't look up.

'Vodka or vodka?' says Jeannie, leading the way to the chairs by the pool.

'Just tonic.'

'As bad as that?' Jeannie raises her eyebrows.

The two women settle on the loungers by the pool. It's so pretty from here at night: the little lights on the beach, the blink of the lighthouse. The darkness is thick and warm as an animal pelt, but up here at least you can breathe. And there is perspective; driving here, as the big car bumped up the road to the promontory – crickets chattering drily in the coarse unseen black grass – Bea imagined the people below, the wreck, the troubles, the whole world, diminishing as in a child's magical story. A game she used to play with Timbo when they looked down from a hill and lifted the roofs like lids off the houses and picked out the people and spied into their secret rooms.

And now she fishes for a cigarette but does not light it, lies back in the lounger, closes her eyes. And says: 'Oh God, Jeannie, I feel like Lady Macbeth.'

'When I sacked Fisk,' says Jeannie, 'he cried. Can you imagine, a grown man, *crying.*'

'Oh yes.'

'You're a sucker, Bea.'

'Jeannie, can I stay here tonight?'

'It's serious then? You'd better have vodka.'

'I think I will.'

Jeannie stands over Bea like a doctor, making sure she drinks up. She refills her glass. As the vodka hits Bea's stomach she feels herself depart from her body. The late departed Beatrice Tyler. She floats.

Jeannie is talking to her. 'If you're breaking up you've got to tell Toby.'

'I don't know what we are doing. I don't know what to tell him.'

'They're tougher than you think, you know – children. When I walked out on Froebl, Perry was four. I felt bad about that for a while. I had access. Then one day Perry called me and said he wouldn't be coming to the sea with me because his father was taking him to Disneyland. He was so goddam *polite.*'

'Timbo's not four.'

'So if only you knew he's probably worrying about how to get rid of *you.* He's going to bed with Mercy, isn't he?'

'I think so. Yes, I'm sure he is.'

'Well then.'

Suddenly Bea is crying. She who never cries is shaken by dry sobs that knife her double then turn to a gale of weeping. Tears for whom – herself, Herman, Timbo? Sarah? Harbinger pegged out above an ant-hill? A young female child in a shallow grave? Her own miscarried children? All Bea knows is that these are old unshed tears that have been put away for years, and put away. Grief shunned and soured, pain evaded, needs blocked, rage denied.

'These damn flies,' says Jeannie. 'Let's go in.'

When she has splashed her face with cold water Bea eats hamburgers with Jeannie in the kitchen – not, thank God, the trompe l'oeil dining room.

'I'm getting rid of all that tacky stuff,' says Jeannie. 'People kept walking into the walls.'

Bea finds she is surprisingly hungry. They eat and drink wine, then they drink more wine. Jeannie tells some funny story about Froebl or Fantl or Fisk. Then she says she'll give the next party, the last party of the season.

Apparently Fantl was a South American politician of German extraction who owned most of Panama, or somewhere, and gave Jeannie zinc mines for her birthday. He had black shining starling hair and a limp from one of many attempts upon his life at the hustings. When Fantl first made love to Jeannie he laid orchids on her pillow, fed her quail and imported chocolate ants. Then he put his teeth in a glass and took off his hair and his tin leg and got into bed.

Bea is astonished to find herself laughing, considering the state she arrived in.

'And what did you do?'

'When I left him I went in the middle of the night. I took his hair and his tin leg and left them in a locker at the airport. I mailed the locker ticket from New York. Is it serious with Herman?'

'I'm not sure it was anything to do with Herman at all.'

When Bea decides she's fine, she'll go home now, Jeannie walks out with her to the car.

'I passed those motorcyclists on the way up,' Bea says, 'they nearly pushed me off the road.'

'They're breaking into houses,' says Jeannie, 'two of the new villas last week. You want to lock up.'

'Oh, we're all right on the beach.'

'You ought to get a gun,' Jeannie yells after her. Bea smiles and waves, shaking her head: no guns.

11

ERIN AMONG THE chaos is more stricken, if anything, than Bea herself. She flaps, a disordered bird, keening for everything broken and spoiled.

The night Bea went to Jeannie's and Herman and Toby were at the Willings's, the Honda gang broke into the Tylers'. Except for a bottle of whisky they took nothing, even money, but they urinated on the carpets and slashed the cushions and the curtains and smashed the glass. Long after everything has been cleared up there are still shards of glass. It is dangerous to walk barefoot. They must have scared the cat because it went missing for four days and came back half-starved. It would allow only Bea to feed it. Somehow they missed the bird on the lawn and superstitiously, as though looking for omens, the Tylers are glad of this.

'I'd feel as though I'd been *violated*!' Erin is puzzled, a little shocked, that Bea seems so cold and odd about it all. What she doesn't know is that Bea, arriving home first, stood alone among the wreckage with glittering eye. Though there is no connection, since Jeannie shot the dog she has been expecting something like this, she has been expecting something like this all summer. She could have thrown back her head, ululated, burned laurel leaves, prophesied. That was how Toby found his mother, glinting like a witch. He was glad of the excuse to run and fetch Herman. When they got back Bea was standing before a cracked mirror, looking like Snow White's stepmother.

All Herman's Mother Carey's chickens come home to roost.

Eventually Herman asked Bea: 'You've called the police?'

'What's the point in calling the police?'

'Because our house has been broken into.'

'If we could get through to the police they wouldn't come. And if they came, what could they do?'

'Burglaries have to be notified.'

'We haven't been burgled.'

For one crazy moment Toby wondered if Bea herself had come back and smashed up the house.

Herman found brandy and they drank it. Toby wished his parents would tell him if they were breaking up and in another way he didn't care; and in another way he didn't want to know because he could not decide what he would feel about it. So he went to bed.

Now the house is more or less straight. In summer they don't need curtains anyway and everyone has been very kind: cushions from Francine, glass from Jeannie and plates from the Bonifaces. Tears from Erin. Erin warns Herman that he should keep an eye on Bea – this kind of thing can affect women deeply, especially at the age we are now. Tears in her eyes, she invites – urges – Bea to cry, to get it out of her system. She is speaking professionally. Bea looks at her blankly and does not tell Erin: I have done my crying.

There is something though in what Erin says. Bea sleeps badly. The porch door latch has not been fixed since the invasion and the slightest air in the night sets it banging. Bea gets up and goes downstairs. In the dark she sits and smokes and prowls her house – the structure is sound, Harry has done the reglazing, yet it seems to her to have become insubstantial, a paper house. She sees that it might pitch and fall, and the October gales would come and the sand would blow through it. The beach-sleepers, maybe, creep in for shelter, lie in this windowless shell and shivering, pull their rags around them. Then even they are gone and the house at last utterly dissolves before sea and sand and time. Underwater weed waves where now I stand, a diver discovers trace fossils, a shard of glass, the shape of rooms. Fish flick among our secrets.

The cat stops Bea's prowling, brushing against her legs, complaining, nearly tripping her. Bea sits in her wooden chair at the kitchen table and thinks: Sarah, bloody Sarah.

When her mother was first ill she said: I am a terminal case. But I have no intention of dying. Which in some way put upon her daughter a terrible load of death.

The porch door crashes. The sea, ebbing, tugs at the shingle, the moon is full.

I remember, I remember.

When her father was alive before her mother was ill the parental home was a place of tidiness and certainties: washed blue curtains blowing in the breeze, orange flowers in a copper bowl on a polished table, lavender in lined drawers, scent of beeswax. Not that Sarah was housewifely – she simply put the house in its place then played bridge in winter, golf in summer. Small and slim, like Bea, she had a tougher, sallower skin and strong wrists: she played golf like a man.

One knew how the world wagged. One didn't make a fuss.

Then this woman who had told her daughter, life is this, life is that – there was Sarah, widowed, refusing to die, weighing no more than seven stone, living alone, gardening, travelling, golfing, whipping round town in her little cream car, living like a tiger. Indomitable spirit they said, but the doctor asked Bea to come and see him and told her: your mother must slow up.

Bea sat on the other side of the desk looking across the desk at the bland man who had summoned her and thought: well, she's dying, that should slow her up.

'You know,' she said. 'It's difficult.'

Then Bea became older than her mother; all the certainties she had ever known were reversed and she was sitting in the car saying agonisingly to Sarah: mother, do you have to drive so fast?

She had handled it all very badly, she could see that now, because she feared the responsibility for Sarah's death (she feared death). The brave, right thing would have been to say straight to Sarah: look, mother, you are dying and perhaps we should try to like one another a little first?

158

But Bea had been inhibited by pity, by convention. And by scruples – it is for our own sakes, she thought, that we, the living, seek to make peace with the dying.

Anyhow, with Sarah, whatever hope was there for anyone, ever, of peace?

Another doctor: Bea remembers exactly the angle at which the sun struck his desk, something spiky about the light, the fact that he wore his watch on his right wrist. This left-handed, exhausted doctor rubbed his eyes, looked at Bea and seemed to decide that this was a reasonably balanced woman who would not cry at him or collapse on him or sweep the papers from his desk or sue him for negligence. So he told her: 'The dying, you know, become reconciled to death. One notices. At a certain point they seem to need to detach themselves and this can be hurtful to those who care for them. Death demands.' Bea realised vaguely that she was being paid a compliment, he was talking to her common-sense. He was picking his words. 'Death demands concentration.'

'She doesn't like being drugged.'

He looked disappointed and a little apprehensive. What had he got here? A crank?

'You realise without the drugs the pain would be intolerable?'

Death is intolerable, Bea meant, she wants to fight it. And if she can't see it, however can she fight it? But Bea said, I understand. And thrice the cock crowed.

How odd, Bea thinks. I have spent half my life fighting my mother in my blood and here I am, a witch in my own house.

Almost, she is there: the point when she can say – well then, so be it.

'I thought I heard the porch door.'

Toby was dreaming of something broken and he woke and heard the porch door crashing.

'Timbo?'

There he stands in the moonlight, jeans pulled on, face furred with sleep.

'Something woke me.'

'It's just the door. Harry will fix it tomorrow. Want some tea?'

Toby shakes his head. He gets some Coke and drinks it from the can, standing, his back resting against the fridge, his weight on one leg. Judging her? Lately he's been wary of her – when she enters a room he ducks his head into a book; they haven't been alone together since the break-in, and that is probably not a coincidence.

Bea smokes and thinks: we used to be able to talk so easily. Everyone said. And I knew – I did know – my fortune, to have a son who is also a friend. Lately, suddenly, this summer, all the important things go unsaid, the air is full of questions that can never be asked. He looks at me as though he expects me to do something mad, he looks like Orestes. She feels she must explain what she is doing in the kitchen at midnight.

'I was thinking of your grandmother. I was thinking I could never talk to her – not properly.' Bea's hand is shaking. Her voice sounds strange in her own ears – pleading. 'I'm sorry about that now. I never knew what she was *like*. Does that sound silly? You know – you think there is all the time in the world, then people die.'

Toby nods. 'I didn't know her very well. She scared me a bit. She used to give me nightmares.'

'Nightmares?'

'There was a story you used to read me about a witch – just an ordinary story. But I got her muddled up with the witch. I didn't like it when she kissed me because the witch in the story had a poison kiss. I used to scrub my face afterwards.'

Toby grins and Bea is first startled, then she begins to laugh.

'My God! The stories we consider suitable for children! I never knew – I had no idea. But I remember that story – you used to ask for it, that was always the story you wanted.'

Toby's face is moonwashed. It seems easier to talk at night.

He has found it difficult lately to look Bea straight in the eye.

'Maybe we need those stories?' he wonders.

'You needed to be *frightened*?'

'Well, life's fairly frightening, isn't it?' His tone is light, but he's thinking something through. 'I mean: you think the best of everyone, and then you're disappointed.'

'And then?'

'You get used to it?' Toby pauses, there is something he can almost catch but he's not quite there, something heard, glimpsed, in the depths of a magical forest, a wedge of fluttering darkness at the corner of his field of vision. Something to do with violence and death. It's here and then it's gone, because his mother is talking, painfully it seems.

'Children and parents. You know, I think they quarrel because the parent is frightened of being found out, after years of pretending this or that. I'm afraid it hasn't been easy for you this summer.' Bea says quickly, before she loses courage: 'You haven't asked but the answer is I don't know if your father and I are breaking up. I think probably not but it's possible. In any case, it's no one's fault. And either way, you must know we love you. You know that?'

'Of course,' Toby says and these are the two bleakest words Bea has ever heard.

When Toby has gone back to bed Bea stays down for a while. She tells the cat: 'Am I such a wicked woman? Am I really so wicked?'

Toby doesn't want to talk to anyone about this, even Mercy. Besides, she has enough troubles, he thinks, without his. He is supposed to be rescuing her. And then, he wonders however he dared cast himself as self-appointed Batman, Orpheus, white knight on charger, St. George to her Una: sometimes he doesn't feel valiant or free at all.

He thinks of fairy stories in reverse: prince into toad; one day in Mercy's arms he fears such a metamorphosis may take place.

He stays in his room and plays his guitar and finds it

absurd that he is full-grown, Mercy's lover, soon to leave home, free to do anything, go anywhere – and the thought that his parents may be breaking up reduces him to a child listening at doors, lying in bed listening and squeezing his eyes not to cry.

It's very hot. Toby lies on his stomach on his bunk and focuses his telescope (his grandfather's telescope) on the beach, where a girl in a green cardigan – the green children paint grass until they learn better – walks on the beach against the sea; and the sea goes on and on into the sky. The sun burns white, the barefoot girl slips off her cardigan and trails it like seaweed – she seems not to have noticed that the beach is spoiled or she has noticed and does not care. The dogs too have learned to dance between the black deadly pools while further up the beach Harry as Hercules continues to remove the top-sand and carry it away.

Toby looks through the wrong end of the telescope: now the girl and Harry and the dogs are insects scratching on the sand. There are no traps. The beach is clean. Nothing happened.

Something happened last night: Bea was trying to explain something. Toby realises she had been on the edge of a confession – something about adult incompetence, about being found out – and he is ashamed to be thankful that his mother stopped short of confession. Bea did not say: I had a lover that winter I went to the museum.

Why shouldn't she?

Because he needs the myth of his parents' happiness even though there was a time he wished his father dead. Perhaps at some point one simply grows out of the idea of marrying one's mother?

If at times in the past Toby felt excluded by their closeness to one another, now he needs Bea and Herman to be happy so that he can leave them. Also so that he can point at them, as statues in a landscape, monuments to hope, and believe that happiness may be possible.

Toby sighs. He hears Bea moving around downstairs in the kitchen and there is something attentive about the way she puts down dishes, shuts the oven door: she is listening to his silence. The girl on the beach has gone. For the first time that summer, Toby misses Tike Willings, contemporary male company, a bit of nonsense, a bit of swagger. He rubs his hand up and down his bare chest, inspects his muscles and feels his body humming with life, such life leaping in him he can hardly bear to be still: he would like to run, break rocks, shout mindlessly, hunt girls with Tike then roar off, witless and free.

He feels sometimes he's never been young. First he was married to his mother, then to Mercy.

Toby goes down to help Harry move the beach. It's hard work. He sweats out some frets. Then he goes to swim at fossil beach and stays to eat with the troglodytes. They serve a slightly moony loving silence and mungo sprouts. They have been making their own mead. Toby drinks and sleeps dreamlessly, wakes with a shock much later, to see the moon rocking in the sky.

This may be the end but Jeannie will still throw the last party, she always has. She will get fireworks, hire a caterer – astonishing how services collapse but luxuries are still available to people like Jeannie.

It is quite serious, this feeling they all have, of their time here running out and there being nowhere to go. In the past there was always somewhere but now the eastern gate has been slammed and every day there are signs of attrition. Small things. Nothing that would worry a starving peasant in India, they agree, and feel ashamed of their unease, therefore do not speak of it very much. People have always felt this, Bea decides. She looks at Herman talking to the bird and thinks, perhaps that's all the so-called midlife climacteric is about – acknowledgement of death. We are realising that we shall not live forever. She is still resolved not to go back to town.

Francine Fox has taken up ballet. She has always had lovely long dancer's legs and now on the educational channel they are actually teaching ballet on television. Harry is busy with his beach-moving, the children are happy with their sand-pit, so each morning when the house is empty she goes to her barre, home-made from a broomstick handle, and practises, as the teacher tells her to do, before the mirror. She is a little wobbly from her breakfast nip of vodka (concealed in a hair tonic bottle in the bathroom cupboard), and at first it is very difficult, but in time she finds herself not panting quite so much and exhorting her body to feats she had never believed possible. How it will ever be woven together into dance she cannot imagine, she despairs sometimes when they show at the end of the programme, *pour encourager*, excerpts from the real thing. But Francine, panting in her leotard, every muscle in her body punished, dreams of some giant leap she might some day make – that is what she wants: to fly. To leap in the air, how wonderful! To leap, leap over walls, into the air, in one leap leaving behind lobsters and all. And they would point and cry: Francine's flying!

Silly, she says to herself, now you really are talking crazily, they put people away for that sort of talk.

But one day she realises she is drinking less, much less, and dancing for the television doesn't seem such a strange way to pass one's life, after all. Her body, she notices too, is firming, her skin clearing, her hair shines.

She puts Merlyn off a couple of times, then finally agrees to meet him in their usual place. But Francine no longer feels abject – she lies on her back but her mind is far away, dancing above them both, in the high cerulean.

Francine dances, Erin paints, Harry moves the beach. The official inquiry into the wreck continues, apparently, but at a metaphysical level, so it seems to those directly affected. One day there will be a verdict from on high, attributing fault, but whatever use will that be to them? The wreck remains, the birds are dead.

12

'A DEAD DOG?'

'In Jeannie's pool.' Herman looks up from his book. Bea is sitting at the other end of the table making lists of things to do if she is really to winter here, on the beach. 'She's going to drain it. There was some blood.' Bea wears her wire-framed spectacles. She wonders about the storm shutters – if she could live behind storm shutters. Bea considers that the others may have got it wrong: things in the outside world, in the city, are certainly unpleasant and close to unendurable, but there is no real reason, given sensible precautions, why one should not go on living here. She sees herself, an old maid, living here, collecting seashells by the sea-shore. She will be regarded as odd and no one will bother her.

Herman is still worried about this dog.

'Did Jeannie shoot it?'

Bea is wondering about getting a cellar dug, stocking it with tins, dried food, bottled water, blankets, camp beds. Ammunition? A sort of fall-out shelter? Guns, she writes and crosses it out. No, no guns. One might turn out to be a killer. She sighs. Is this list a fantasy?

'Shoot what?'

'The dog.'

'Oh no. No, no one shot it as far as I know. It's throat was cut. It was probably one of the beach-dogs.'

It's hot. There are electrical storms almost every night. Herman puts down his book and goes out to see the bird, his bird. It knows him now and screeches for grapes whenever he approaches the cage. Herman realises that soon he must release it but he is reluctant to let it go, for the bird's sake and for his own. He has come to regard the bird as a friend, and as a talisman, something lucky.

'They're polite to each other,' Toby tells Mercy when she asks. 'Cold war.'

'You don't want to talk about it?'

He shrugs. They are walking along by the sea, Worthy at their heels. 'Not much.'

Mercy nods. 'I've missed you,' she says, looking away from him, then she turns, saying something that has clearly been in her mind and takes courage to bring out: 'I don't want to be a charity, you know.' When Toby tries to protest, she silences him and speaks like a child who has been learning some difficult lesson she is determined to deliver: 'No, I'm much better, really. I've been thinking about this. What I mean is, you don't have to treat me carefully. I shan't fall apart.' They have reached the boathouse. Mercy sits on a rock and Toby sits on another rock, wondering what on earth he is going to say. Has she heard about his night with the troglodytes? Does he love her? However do you know if you love someone? Worthy lowers himself carefully onto a dry, clean patch of sand like an old man into a club chair. He looks at Mercy, then he looks at Toby, and puts his nose on his paws.

Toby looks down. He sees that she has been biting her nails again and looking at her poor, bitten hand, feels himself to be the most callous creature on earth – and he wants to take that hand and kiss it and declare and protest; and in another way, he imagines himself just walking away from her, packing a bag and strolling out of this story. He could do anything. He could live with the troglodytes or walk round the world.

Mercy's still talking.

'I haven't told you the whole truth,' she says. 'I was underground.'

For a moment Toby has no idea what she means. He thinks of graves and tunnels.

'I got mixed up,' Mercy says. 'Well, I got involved with this cell who were going to assassinate someone. It's easy, you know. You feel a bit lost, and someone's nice to you. Then you get to depend on them and then they say, look, we're going to kill this person . . . it just seemed something quite ordinary, as we were all living then. Can you understand that?'

'I think so. I'm not sure.'

'Now I look back, it was all so cold-blooded – not like Erin saving the whale or even what I've heard about Paris '68. Everything was organised: timetables, plans, maps, safe houses, signals. No one knew anyone else's real name.'

'Who were they? Irish? Arabs?'

'No, that was the thing – there seemed no political motive, not even anarchy. They were very pure, pure killers. It was weird, creepy . . . it was that boy from the hospital I told you about who took me to them, the one who killed himself. Anyhow, it was nice for a while, just to be accepted as not crazy, and I only had a very small job to do but suddenly I realised I couldn't possibly do it. Yet I felt frightened they wouldn't let me out, and guilty because these people were my friends, so I simply stopped eating again. I was lucky – it was called off, and none of us knew enough about the whole plot to give away the others. They let me go.'

'Poor love.' Toby is shattered but tries not to show it. He touches her cheek, almost shyly: Mercy is only one year older and yet she makes him feel such an innocent. He feels he's been pathetically naif, imagining he can just turn his back on violence, refuse to know it, walk away. Then he thinks maybe at some level of his mind he'd guessed about Mercy – he remembers that hallucination the night of the conversation with Bea: the wedge of fluttering darkness like a sooty feather. At the time Toby had supposed this had something to do with his grandmother, but now he wonders.

'Oh, I'm fine,' says Mercy. 'I got away.' She sits, shoulders slumped, on the rock, looking out at the sea. It is so hot, so still, a skin seems to have been stretched over the ocean, there is no movement on the surface at all. 'Looking back though. As I've said, the frightening thing is, given a certain frame of mind, how ordinary and easy it seems to kill. You think someone deserves to die – which he did – and from there the next step, the killing, is reasonable, logical.'

'No,' says Toby, 'no, I can't see that. Not the killing.'

But then, he thinks, I might feel differently if I had parents like Mercy's who were always trying to kill each other? His own, he knows, if they do break up will make sure the end is bloodless. Though lately he has sensed some violence in Bea, they have always set great store by courtesy. In other people's houses he's heard such ranting and raving – his parents' has seemed sometimes to Toby the only gentle relationship in the world: a herbivore marriage. If they could be charged with anything it might be that they have brought him up sequestered from the facts of life. If he were to cry *j'accuse*, it would be to say: why didn't you tell me it would be so rough? That there would be pain to be dealt with, and fear and rage?

Toby tries to imagine Mercy among the killers. He sits on his rock and does not know what to say, how to console her. Even if he wants to console her. She has revealed herself (like his mother) as a bird of a dangerous feather.

'I'm trying to imagine it,' he says awkwardly. Oh Lord, what a prig he feels – whoever is he, knowing nothing, to set himself up as judge? And poor Mercy, chewing her nails, how could she ever have been anything but victim?

Unless – it occurs to Toby, as an unformed, barely formulated idea – victims conspire at their own doom. He'd seen it at school: the boy who is picked on inviting torment almost smilingly. Anything better than nonentity. Nothing worse than loneliness.

This is as far as he can go now. If he were different – like Tike – Toby would simply have a wonderful summer making love to Mercy, even boasting to himself about it – kiss and tell; if he were older or wiser or braver he would know how to help her, he would put her experience in its place, make some sense for her of her confusion.

As it is, Toby picks up a pebble and flings it as far as he can, startling Worthy. There is too much hidden, Toby thinks savagely, there are too many secrets. Nowadays parents (though not, thank God, his) walk around naked in front of their children, officially there is open government – but what really matters buried, whispered, folded away, the hate, the folly, the pain. He knows now for certain, as though he had seen it written down, that his parents' marriage is not the fairy tale he has been brought up to believe. Bea did sleep with someone else that winter she went to the museum. She probably hated her mother. Herman is full of fear, he let his own father die alone.

It will take Toby a while to accept his parents' incompetence. It is as though someone had been reading him a story – like a fairy story, a formula that stuck to certain anticipatable rules – and then quite suddenly, without warning, the characters jump out of their roles: the good fairy reveals herself as the wicked witch of the west; it is no longer sure that endings will be happy.

'They don't know,' Mercy says. 'They'd make such a fuss, so you won't tell them? Anyhow, it's all over.'

'Of course not.'

'I don't think they could cope with it.'

In accord at last, they smile as if to say: parents are pretty hopeless.

Jeannie's party hangs over them all. Only Erin is really keen, because she loves other people's parties. For the rest it is mostly a ritual to be observed. A little more than that this time perhaps – the break-in at the Tylers' has disturbed them all; the wreck and the pollution of their precious bay was bad enough but viewed sensibly might be taken as an act of God, like the weather. The break-in struck deeper. Erin was not the only one to feel this as a violation, an assault on the identity itself. As Jeannie remarked, one of the penalties of middle-age is that you mind being burgled.

So maybe, even those who grumble most about it need this party. Like many of nature's arrangements, they have both their individual identities and a social, corporate one. At times of stress it is their instinct to herd.

In a complex organism, thinks Herman, each cell functions by grace of the rest. The Company, for instance, appears despotic yet it is no stronger, no *realler*, than the sum of its parts. It depends entirely upon the replaceability of those parts, which means that in a real sense it does not exist. He finds the thought cheering, quite heady. Once it would have frightened him to death, so this must be an improvement?

If you look at it like that – he tells his friend, the bird in the cage – the Company's no more than an idea. All we have to do is say poof and it's dead.

The trouble is, Herman supposes, we would all have to say poof at the same time, or it wouldn't work? Yet the fact remains, the Company is a figment of our imaginations: its reality depends upon the suspension of our disbelief.

The bird has become bored. It is exploring its armpit, if birds had armpits.

'Well,' says Herman, 'I suppose we'll have to let you go soon.' He broods now about this suspension of disbelief business – has he invented the Company or has the Company invented him? Life once was very simple, the issues – even if he ducked them – were clear; it has become so complicated now, everything has implications, there are about five hundred angles to every question. And at the same time it is very simple. When you come down to it, what we're all after, if we told the truth, is pleasure. Not happiness – no one knows what that is – but gratification. And we spend most of our lives in fear – positive fear of disaster, negative fear that gratification will elude us.

Herman sighs and opens the door of the cage. 'Come on,' he says, 'come out, you're all right – you can fly.' The bird at last steps out, looks round, sees no grapes, pecks Herman and goes back in.

Toby is sorry for his father. Or rather he is, with some embarrassment, making some attempt to understand him. Bea's mood has inevitably thrust them together. At first this was awkward, now it has half-blossomed into a companionable relationship. They don't talk very much but they trail the lugger round to unpolluted fossil beach and go sailing. One evening they take a tent and camp out. Herman cooks. Nothing important is said but for a few hours they are quite happy.

Jeannie's party: suddenly it seems a very good idea. They need distracting and whatever you say about Jeannie's parties, they are never dull. In the first place she is rich, in the second she is inventive.

'But I've got a creepy feeling about it,' confesses Erin, 'in my knees. I suppose it's psychosomatic.'

Bea smiles. 'That's the Irish in you.'

'Oh, that was years ago.' Erin sucks the sharp end of her paintbrush. She is painting Bea sitting in the rocker on the Tylers' porch. Behind her, on the ledge, two pots of geraniums and the cat sun themselves. Erin has painted these – the whole of the background, in fact – in great detail. The only empty space in the picture is Bea herself, still no more than a ghostly outline. The truth is, Erin is having trouble with her vision of Bea: today there seems to be something sharp, something jagged in the space her friend should fill. 'I mean,' Erin continues, troubled, frowning at her painting with ferocious concentration, 'the blood, yes – but I've never even been to Ireland. Anyhow, I always get these feelings about parties, and I always enjoy them – other people's, anyway. When I was a child I adored parties, but every time I was sick before I went.' How difficult it is, thinks Erin, to hold on to one's vision long enough to get it down on canvas; she knows what she sees but is so often disappointed in the result. There is however, sometimes, a moment of rare, unalloyed happiness, when she comes upon a canvas she did years ago pushed in the back of a cupboard and brings it out into the light of day and sees that it is good. If Merlyn does not chop her up with an axe, or she does not polish off herself, Erin might be found, towards the end of her life, a fat lady on a camp stool on this same beach, humming as she paints.

Perhaps she will paint Bea collecting seashells by the seashore. Two old women.

Erin smiles: 'I was thinking, it will be lovely if you stay for the winter. It's quite different though, you know – very cold. It gets colder, just as the summers get hotter. Something to do with the polar ice-cap, Harry says. Melting.'

'I'm not sure,' says Bea, 'nothing's settled.'

At that moment the crazy cat leaps and settles. And suddenly, just as she is about to put away her brushes, Erin has her vision of Bea in the picture, as though she had never known her at all: a wild woman in a rocking-chair, with a cat on her lap.

A scent of meat and of something dying. Money: a lot of money at Jeannie's and also putrefaction. Her tropical garden, presumably, unless, as someone remarks, Jeannie has chopped up a husband and planted him. And now, with the beauty of the orchids, there is a queer stench of death.

Well, everyone drinks quite a lot.

The orchids are admired.

'Jeannie – you look fan-tastic!'

So she does, in peacock. Breastless as a soldier, her face and throat the colour of tanned hide, the texture of reptile, her hands grave-spotted, her stride graceless – yet in the peacock shift of silk like tissue, shot with silver thread, rings on almost every finger of her short, serviceable hands, there is no one like Jeannie (thank God, some might say). She creates her own force-field. The air around her crackles.

Though they swear they won't, people always dress up for Jeannie's parties.

Francine wears a tube of flame, flounced at the ankle, low-cut and zipped at the back, she walks like a candle, a tapering light. Drinks only Perrier.

'What's Francine on?' hisses Jeannie.

'Ballet,' says Bea. 'She's stopped drinking and dances for the television every day.'

'I always said that girl was crazy. What if there's a power cut?'

'Then she'll dance by herself, I suppose.'

'Is she still sleeping with Merlyn Willings?'

'For heaven's sake, Jeannie, I don't know. And keep your voice down.'

'Why? Everyone knew, didn't they? They might as well have done it on the beach. They did do it on the beach.'

'Jeannie, you're salacious.'

'I still say she's high, the silly bitch.'

Jeannie's party is catered, of course, expensively. Various seamanlike-looking persons in matelot sweaters (Jeannie's lovers?) serve food and drink. Erin has discovered the garlic dip and her eyes shine. Whatever misgivings she had about this party seem to be dispelled, and everyone feels much the same. There is this queer smell but there is also lushness paid for by Jeannie's money. They feel stroked, pleasantly slumberous, and all exclaim at Jeannie's new décor, revealed tonight for the first time: the trompe l'oeil has gone and in place of it each of the large, high-ceilinged rooms is lined with large mirrors flanked by candelabra; so that there appears to be, beside and beyond the real party, a second, mirrored party going on of people so much more beautiful than themselves, dancing and smiling and talking brilliantly beyond a hedge of flaming candles. Almost, they can admire themselves in these dancers and talkers, phantasms. In this light the mirrors look like a skin through which they could easily pass out of their human troubles: the fact that they are not so young, that they will die, that their bones sometimes ache. They dance and dance, these wonderful mirror people, to invisible music.

There are strangers, Jeannie's other guests, the rich. They don't dance so much but sit at little gilt tables. The men don't talk. The women preen and glitter and chatter and kiss, first upon one cheek, then upon the other: they have had tucks taken in their breasts, their bottoms, their faces. There is a woman who looks like a fox, another laughs like a tropical bird. Tomorrow they will be gone, in the white motor-yacht anchored in the bay (it is not certain that they were real in the first place).

Bea remembers the flash of a yellow bird in the ruined conservatory, before Jeannie came.

'There was a bird,' she says, 'and a spotted toad.'

Erin wrinkles her nose. 'That smell?'

Herman dances with Francine. He feels odd and wonders if Jeannie could have spiked the canapés?

'Herman,' says Francine, dozing beautifully on his shoulder, 'you are a good man, the only good man I know.'

He feels her tongue flick his ear.

'Don't do that, Francine.'

'You're a lovely, lovely man.'

'Francine,' says Herman, gently but firmly, 'you must stop behaving like this.'

'It's so hot, isn't it? I think I'll go for a swim.' And off she goes, walking through the party like a wand. Herman will remember how she looked, and wonder if he should have stopped her. If he could.

Does one ever forget? Bea is sitting at one of the tables between the fox-woman and an interior decorator. She remembers everything. She is tired of remembering, yet it appears to be a necessary process if one is to go on. She sees a handsome couple dancing in the mirror and it takes her a moment to realise that this is Herman, her husband, dancing with Francine.

'Asparagus.'

The fox-woman and the interior decorator, who wears a gold bracelet round his ankle, talk through Bea as though she were not there. They are talking about asparagus and some-one called Dodo and someone called Frank. Interesting, thinks Bea, plucking at a thread in her skirt, how the very rich survive, whatever.

Remember.

She remembers how, when his father was dying and Sarah too, Herman was in Madrid, then he came back with chicken-pox that turned out to be shingles. When her mother died he was in New York and on the plane back to his father's funeral had an attack, what appeared to be a heart attack but was later diagnosed as tachycardia, a faltering of the beat. Bea met him at the airport, propped up on a stretcher, and saw the terror of death in his face. No organic causes. This terror lasted long after it had been confirmed that there were no organic causes. He was afraid to be alone. At his father's funeral Bea thought Herman was about to faint and topple into the open grave. Patiently, gently, she had relayed to him the verdict: no organic cause (meaning, you are fit to get up and go to your father's funeral). She had been nice to him. She had been monstrous.

When Sarah was buried Bea had not shed a tear but she wanted to shout: Come back! Come back – we haven't finished!

Fireworks are announced.

'I'm sorry,' says Bea, 'I thought you said you were an interior decorator?'

'Actually, I used to be a masseur and now I'm an acu-puncturist.'

'That must be very interesting.'

'It's very expensive.'

'Don't listen to him,' says the fox-woman, 'he's a faggot.'

'Does it work?'

'Sometimes.'

'I hate faggots,' says the fox-woman to no one in particular.

'Shut up, you cow.'

The fox-woman weeps. She sits there, smoking and drink-ing, the tears running down her face. 'I want to go home!'

'Come on!' says Erin, 'there are going to be fireworks!'

Bea looks for Herman. She sees the top of his head but can't reach him because of the crush to get onto the terrace for the

175

fireworks. There is nothing worse, she thinks, than fear, yet that too we must face: everyone is more or less frightened. They put a red blanket over Herman on the stretcher when she met him at the airport and she rode with him in the ambulance to the hospital; all the time Bea remembered the fire-extinguisher in the museum where she had met Harbinger, and the poinsettia in Sarah's sick-room, every time she looked at the red blanket. She hates red. It is the colour of death. When she miscarried there was so much blood.

But the fireworks: they are beautiful. Everyone sees them from his own point of view. In Jeannie's watch-tower Toby asks Mercy to go away with him. Bea finds Herman, and he smiles, and takes her hand and they stand there, holding hands, like children. Only Worthy Willings on the beach cowers in his basket as the lightning cracks and the rockets bloom.

Francine stands on the diving board and unzips, kicks off her dress and for a moment stands naked then leaps as the sparks fall down.

'No,' says Mercy to Toby in the tower. 'You're saying that for the wrong reasons: because you're sorry for me, or you're in a panic. Anyway, I'm not quite sure I'm ready to live with anyone.'

Toby kisses her shoulder and turns his face away. At last he admits to himself what he feels: relief.

No one misses Francine for some time. They are used to her disappearing at parties to share a cloak-cupboard with Merlyn or a bed or a bathroom. But Merlyn is there being talked at by Betty Boniface about the re-birth of the novel (a speculation inspired by her own parturition?). So where is Francine?

They find her towards dawn, broken in the drained pool, where the dog died. She leapt. She fell, she falls, she was always falling, falling.

13

THE WEATHER BREAKS. The rain at this season is nowadays almost tropical. Violent downpour followed by brief sun in which everything steams: mould grows in closets and on books, milk turns sour and – a painful irony – Jeannie's pool fills. The young take no notice of the rain. Their elders, minimally clothed beneath, sweat in oilskins and arrive at each other's houses dressed like lifeboatmen. There is a lot of visiting, what with the public enquiry into the wreck continuing, the official inquest into Francine's death and the private, grief-torn speculation.

No one actually says what they all feel: Francine was not the expected victim. Mercy or Erin, yes – either of them might have ducked out of life any time, but Francine had been so much better lately? And anyhow, in spite of all her dramas, she had never seemed the type. Some people simply aren't.

It is Jeannie, as usual, who first speaks the unspeakable, and, in a way, this is a relief to them all, to have it said.

'I knew she was dumb, but I didn't think she was that kind of idiot.'

'But Jeannie,' says Erin, 'we don't *know* what happened. It was dark and maybe no one told her the pool was drained? I mean, she always loved diving, you remember? And then taking off her dress, she might have tripped – all those flounces round the hem. Perhaps she just climbed to the board, and then decided she wanted to swim?'

Herman says: 'There'll be the coroner's verdict'. Even as he speaks he knows what it will be. They all do.

From Harry, Bea learns the true meaning of the word inconsolable. She is shamed, feels she has been selfish lately, inturned: Harry's grief puts all their small sorrows in the shade.

Erin has the little Foxes most of the day. Bea drives Harry into the town to deal with the apparatus of death: police, coroner, undertaker. Then he says he wants to be left alone, but on an impulse, after a day of wondering, Bea rings him, gets no reply, dons her oilskins and tramps through the rain to the Foxes'. Harry, the practical man who abhors chaos, sits at the kitchen table surrounded by dirty crockery from the children's breakfasts. Bea hangs up her oilskin, washes up, takes silent Harry into the sitting-room and pours a large brandy for each of them.

After a long time he finally says: 'I don't know how you get through this sort of thing.' And then: 'It makes no difference but I keep wondering why.'

'I think.' Bea looks at her glass. The worst things are the signs of Francine's presence no one has brought themselves to remove: the barre, the mirror. Francine has passed through the mirror. 'I think,' she says with an effort: 'she just decided it was time to go. Perhaps people feel that sometimes. Not exactly suicide, not exactly accident. There's a sort of grey area between.'

She gets up to refill their glasses and her hand brushes Harry's, by accident; he grasps and clings to it. At last he weeps, a gale of weeping.

Bea stays with him all that day and it is like living with a madman. At one point he flings his glass at the mirror, another time he buries his head in her lap then he goes to the streaming window and crashes his skull against it. He sleeps for a while and wakes crying. Bea holds him and rocks him. There is so much violence, it is hard to believe one room could contain it. The room might implode. Bea rings Erin to keep the children and rings Herman, then she stays most of the night with Harry, drinking with him, failing to persuade him to eat, watching while he sleeps, keeping watch for him to wake and rage. About dawn she goes home and shivers in Herman's arms.

The season is ending. One night, Bea wakes, alert, sensing something. She's cold, she gets up to fetch a blanket, wraps it round her shoulders and stands at the window: there is a raking sound of the sea combing the shingle, the blind rattles, the porch door is flapping. She goes downstairs to lock the door and finds Timbo in the kitchen making a sandwich.

'Poor Harry never did fix that door. The wind's changed.'

He nods. 'It woke me.'

Bea gets herself a glass of milk. The cat swears at her. She pours beer into its saucer, then she sits at the table, still shivering. She remembers when she was a madwoman in this kitchen, remembering too much, another night scene with Timbo. But she had to remember.

'It's a gale out there – we'll have to put up the storm shutters soon. There used to be wreckers on this coast, you know.' But she likes this weather, Bea thinks, she looks forward to the winter, the storms, the taste of salt, the difficulties. 'I think I'll stay, for a while anyway.'

Timbo is still a little wary of her. He eats his sandwich, then he looks at his plate. 'I'll be going.'

'I know.'

'Mercy knows a place teaching English in Japan.'

'She'll go with you?'

'No.'

Bea washes her glass and his plate, very thoroughly, as though it were important to get them clean. Toby's saying something.

'But I'm not sure about you alone here.'

'I won't be,' Bea says gently. 'Not all the time. I'll go to town and your father will come here. We haven't talked about it, but that's what will happen. It's funny' – she tries to explain – 'marriages have a way of mending themselves, without anyone saying anything. They change, but sometimes they mend.' In saying this, she realises it is true.

Toby feels as though he had been holding his breath and now can let it out. He wants to whoop and dance, he loves this cold scourging air that blows through the house. In Japan he'll miss that: this coast is grained in him. But he goes to bed grinning: free, he tells himself – lying sleepless on his bunk in the room his parents made for him – with one bound I am free!

Then he is sad for a while, because it seems to him that happiness is always qualified, there is always the pull of one need against the tug of another. Toby falls asleep at last, hushed by the wind and the tide going out tugging at the sinking land, hushed, shushed.

In the morning the windows are stained with salt. Sand has blown onto the porch and the same wind seems to have whipped away the beach-dogs.

'Where are the dogs?' Bea wonders.

'Gone to town,' says Jeannie, 'good riddance.'

'A lot of them die in the winter,' says Erin in a small voice.

Bea's not sorry to see the back of the dustbin raiders and yet, she thinks, the beach is not the same without their strange dances and waving tails. Worthy's pleased, naturally, to be rid of those feral and disturbing scents – ears windblown, he escorts the women quite friskily along the reclaimed beach. The cat follows at a distance on fastidious, high-stepping paws: the stench of oil still interferes with its proper hunting; the dead fish that were washed up after the leak decay uselessly at high-water mark.

'There's nothing wrong with that dog,' says Jeannie. 'Cardiac nothing.'

'But that's the *point*,' Erin protests. 'He just thought he had. The vet said.'

'Then send him to a dog shrink.'

Erin says nothing, but later she confides in Bea: 'Jeannie Fisk really is a wicked woman.'

'She was joking, Erin.'

'Oh. Oh, I do *wish* I had a sense of humour!'

'I got through to the Catarullas,' says Bea, 'but they weren't there. I mean,' she tells Herman, 'the line has been re-connected but there's no reply.' She wonders vaguely what has happened to their summer tenants in the city. Have they been mugged to death? Has the house burned down? Though Herman will go there soon, the city seems to her quite unreal. She walks with her husband on the beach and the spume stings her face wonderfully. This season of the year confirms in her that she is a Protestant of the northern hemisphere. A violent woman too, in some ways monstrous, but she can accept that now and take into her spirit Sarah; also Harbinger and the death he would have found anyway, even without her; and her dead children. Not Francine, quite yet.

Yes, she can live here quite well.

'Is it true,' Bea says companionably, 'the oil's running out?'

'Yes.'

Then she'll be a woman collecting driftwood on the sea-shore. Herman will come down sometimes. They could make a last stand here.

The summer people go away. The Bonifaces. Harry and the little Foxes.

Harry, in fact, plans to sell up. One day while he's out, at his request the women go in and clear out Francine's things to give to charity. It's a sad job, a terrible one, invading the intimacy of drawers and cupboards and closets. They feel like grave-robbers. At least there are no papers. There was always a joke that Francine could not read – perhaps she couldn't write, either. Oddly, Harry and Merlyn Willings get on better than they have for a long time: they jog together before breakfast, two widowers by a grey sea.

And Herman, early one bright morning, releases his bird, insisting this time, shutting the cage door behind it. Out-raged, it flaps its wings and sulks.

'No,' says Herman firmly, 'off you go. Shoo!'

When it becomes clear that there are to be no more grapes the bird takes off, at last, into the wind, uncertainly at first, then flying steadily, riding the thermals – with hardly a flick of the wing, just the gentlest and most effortless adjustment, the bird sails off into the dangerously brilliant day. And Herman watches until it's out of sight. He feels like Daedalus. And then he feels a flick of joy that doesn't last but may return. The sun is already fading to a dirty lemon as the day's rain arrives. Herman gazes out across the bay. The water darkens beneath the running cloud. He sees a little boat with brown sails heeling and tacking, and wonders who would have taken out the lugger on a day like this?

Mercy reads to Merry and the little Foxes on the Tylers' porch.

"The earth came into being about 4,500 million years ago. Little is known about any life on Earth during the first 4,000 million years." The glass doors of the porch are closed and in here it is quite cosy. Bea sits sewing in the rocking chair, Worthy asleep at her feet and the geranium cuttings ranged behind her on the shelf. This winter, she thinks, since she'll be here to tend her cuttings, she'll get a greenhouse heater. She loves the calmness of geraniums, their sharp peppery scent, their furry leaves, their crayon colouring. Like smoked salmon, she thinks, it's a taste one develops with age along with an appetite for autumn. Spring grows noisy and obvious, unkind as a mirror.

Mercy has become so beautiful this summer, it's hard to remember the starveling she was.

The children fidget. They can't take in 4,500 million years – who can? Mercy distracts them with the pictures but sea urchins bore them and so do ammonites. They find Eryops eating a giant dragonfly more interesting but it is the dinosaurs that catch, at least for a moment, their flickering attention. The information that they died out (like Francine) is received calmly enough. Merry says her gerbil died out (like Francine). 'It got broken. Can we watch telly?'

Mercy smiles and shrugs. The children go indoors.

The woman and the girl sit in the gale-lashed porch-room. There has been sun earlier but now the windows stream and

Bea, her hands resting on her sewing, her gaze fixed on the tumbling bay, wishes this season would be over and the true winter would come, they would all be away, leaving her in possession of this place, of herself.

'I think it's settled lower,' she says, 'the wreck.'

'But it's still there.'

'Yes.'

'You'd think it would have broken up. Isn't it strange: it's been there so long we hardly notice it.' They sit quietly for a time, then Mercy goes on: 'There's something I want to ask you, Bea. D'you think my mother will be all right if I go? She *seems* better and Merlyn's being quite nice to her at the moment. I mean he's not hitting her any more and she's painting a lot. I think she ought to have a show.'

'So do I. Don't worry, I'll keep an eye on Erin. But where will you go?'

'Oh – back to town I suppose. I'll finish my course. I'll get a proper flat and a job if I can.' Mercy frowns slightly. She is concentrating, trying to explain something, wondering if there is anything to explain. Bea remembers her on the way to the lighthouse island: violets, all violets, something tenuous and dreaming, the crazy hat, the trailing hand – and now this pensive phantasm has become a strong, sensible young woman, talking about jobs and flats. 'You see, it sounds silly, but I have this feeling that I want to live an *ordinary* life – work, friends, shopping, cooking, marriage even? I feel I can do this now. Maybe the city's not the place any more but I have to start somewhere.'

Bea remembers her in the hospital, begging her, bullying her to eat, to live. 'You can manage?'

Mercy knows what they are talking about. 'Oh, yes, don't worry, I can manage quite well. I'm not crazy any more.'

'You never were.'

When Mercy leaves to take the children home, Bea asks her to wait a moment, goes to her fossil drawer and puts in Mercy's hand – closing the girl's fingers over it – Aporrhais, her favourite, her daughter. 'Please.' Don't say anything, she means, but keep it.

'Look,' says Mercy, 'someone's out in the lugger. It must be Toby.'

When they have gone, Bea looks out across the bay and sees not the storm, nor the lugger, but another boat always making a vanishing landfall that is never made, and a girl in a foolish hat, trailing her hand in the water.

Toby is leaving tomorrow, with Herman. He takes the lugger out for the last time, in the shining early morning; everything seems fresh: the sky washed, the waves clean at last slapping the hull and breaking white over the bows as he goes about. As he goes about, the sky heels and the earth dips, saucer-shaped, containing the bay, the bay is contained even as the sky darkens and the wind freshens: the lugger can manage this sea easily. Outside, as the storm mounts, it would be a struggle but the bay contains the violence.

Toby cannot imagine Japan.

Go on, said his mother, the first time he sailed to the island.

He is leaving.

The sea, when he turns and runs, is a different animal, no longer dancing and tossing but a serious slow-mounting beast that gathers secretly astern and just as it seems about to mount and swamp the little boat, holds her seemingly help-less for the moment in which he may adjust the tiller, then lets her slide down and away and on, off the grey cliff of a wave. While the sea humps beneath her and runs away harmlessly.

Marriages mending, thinks Toby. His mother says the marriage is mended and he hopes that is true because he needs it to be true. (There is that unexpected rock, invisible at high water. You can go aground here, hole your vessel, without local knowledge. Toby gybes and the boom swings across, the mast shudders but will not snap.)

He would go now anyway.

There comes a point – and he has reached it – when all the reasons in the world won't keep you, even though you can give no reason for going. To think, to strut a bit round the world or sit around until you have found your own reasons, or that there are no reasons any more.

It's a full gale now. Toby eases the sheets, shivers and hunches low, prepared for an uncontrolled gybe. The houses on the beach look miles away and small and frail. The water is black, bitterly cold as the odd rogue wave leaps aboard and finds him out. Toby has the sense of the strong little boat tugging at the reins and he eases the sheets again and lets her run. It's such a marvellous wild ride he feels sad that it must ever finish and at the same time he yells as she kicks up her stern and carries him on; she is dancing, and singing in her rigging. A driving force.

14

AND THEN THERE are Erin and Bea. Erin has decided to give up her post but Merlyn is back at college, though not quite the goat he used to be, since Francine's death, Jeannie has gone wherever people like Jeannie go in the winter and the house on the promontory is empty and shuttered. One of her matelots has drained her pool of the autumn floods and, now it is winter, sweeps it clear of fallen leaves.

The verdict on Francine was suicide and only Erin still finds it necessary or even possible to invent another ending for Francine. Sometimes she walks along the beach to Bea's in the afternoon, a touching, weird and stumpy figure in full-length oilskin, matching hat and waders, often carrying her painting equipment under her arm. She likes painting in Bea's porch-room, with the greenhouse heater.

Her pictures have changed lately. She seems to be getting them from inside her head and they hover somewhere just between her earlier photographic technique and the abstract. They were never large but now they grow smaller and smaller, and all are of some remembered or imagined summer: beaches, pools, sun, blocks of pink and orange and staring blue. The figures, she says, she will put in later when she knows who they are. The windows are blind with salt and Erin sits in Bea's porch-room painting summer with her tongue stuck out like a child at a drawing lesson.

'But anyone could make that mistake in the dark. How was Francine to know the pool had been drained?'

'They didn't seem to think it was normal to climb to a high diving board wearing a very expensive dress. Unless one happened to be drunk or drugged. And Francine was neither that night, for a wonder. Evidence was given.'

Erin protests. 'But why then? If she *had* been stoned I could understand.'

Bea picks her words carefully, trying to explain what she said to Harry and bearing in mind that not so long ago Erin herself had seemed the most popular candidate for suicide. 'I think she just saw the door to go out and took it.'

'But she was so beautiful!'

Erin doesn't come for a couple of days. Then turns up in a full gale, excited and mysterious. She lays out on the Tylers' floor the series of small, square paintings.

'They're perfect,' says Bea. She looks closer. At first she imagines it to be a seagull then she understands that the figure that links the sequence is a woman, flying upwards.

Winter. Weather is king. The sea searches them out and all their habitations, driving salt past their defences, ripping the storm shutters from the hinges in the houses of the summer people where there is no one left to repair and shore up. The troglodytes are gone and a woman walks on the beach, collecting wood, an eccentric figure.

The wreck remains. They have the verdict now.

Human error.

Bea, waiting for Herman, looks out towards the island and thinks, well, that's finished and it will be difficult now. Her skin is rimed in the salt wind, the girl of violet shades and the boy on the dark water are forever there, and they are gone. I shall die, Herman too, one way or another – there is so much violence about, there always has been: nothing special about this.

Meanwhile, it could be – wonderful?